Also by Guy Browning

The Social Survival Handbook
Double Your Salary, Bonk Your Boss, Go Home Early
Innervation: Creativity from the Inside
Weak at the Top
Grass Roots Management
Never Hit a Jellyfish With a Spade
Never Push When It Says Pull
Office Politics
The Lost Pond
The Pocket Guru
Maps of My Life
How to be Normal
The British Constitution: First Draft

DISCARDED

My Life in Lists

My Life in Lists

Guy Browning

■ SQUARE PEG

10 9 8 7 6 5 4 3 2 1

Square Peg, an imprint of Vintage,
20 Vauxhall Bridge Road,
London SW1V 2SA

Square Peg is part of the Penguin Random House
group of companies whose addresses can be found at
global.penguinrandomhouse.com.

Penguin
Random House
UK

www.vintage-books.co.uk

A CIP catalogue record for this book is available
from the British Library

ISBN 9781910931585

Printed and bound in Great Britain by Clays Ltd, St Ives plc

Penguin Random House is committed to a sustainable future
for our business, our readers and our planet. This book is
made from Forest Stewardship Council® certified paper.

MIX
Paper from
responsible sources
FSC® C018179

To Ceci, Theo and Will

Helpful Things to Know About This Book

1. I started writing these lists when I was 10.

2. Just after we'd studied the Ten Commandments at school.

3. I thought if God can say it all in 10 points so can I.

4. My mother always badgered me to keep a diary.

5. Because she always wished she'd kept a diary.

6. My dad preferred To Do lists because he was an engineer.

7. These lists were a kind of compromise.

8. I suppose these are my private To Do lists.

9. Except they are about what actually got done.

10. Let's call them my What Actually Happened lists.

What I Will Do When I Am Grown Up

1. Marry a tall woman from distant Ophir.*

2. Travel around the world with porters and leather luggage.

3. Drive at 90mph in a blue Jensen Interceptor.

4. Have two of each type of children to be fair on everyone.

5. Buy my mum and dad a Georgian mansion with a range of servants.

6. Build a secret tunnel with lighting between my garden and Steve's house.

7. Set up a new nice political party called the Quiet Life Party.

8. Invent a new flavour like liquorice but less disgusting.

9. Run a mile in under three minutes.

10. Have my sisters emigrated for their own good.

* Place from my dad's favourite poem which he recites every Christmas.

My Friends in Mr Bennett's Class

1. Steve Baker is my best friend. He lives five houses away.

2. Alex Cartwright is very clever and very polite. But lies.

3. Lance Adams is brilliant at football and has toys with batteries.

4. Ben Sandford has glasses and protractors and says weird things.

5. Leon Lawrence has long hair like his dad and listens to rock.

6. Becky Hatton has dark hair and braces and a bra.

7. Michael Thompson has curly black hair and red cheeks and fleas.

8. Paul Jenkins is short and ordinary and always has a black comb.

9. Ruth Simons is annoying but her mum is best friends with my mum.

10. Emma Standish has long blonde hair and runs fast. I secretly love her.

How I Described My Family in My 'Describe Your Family' Project

1. My dad is an engineer who builds tunnels. He is like a mole.

2. When he's at home he likes to dig in his vegetable garden.

3. My mum says he plants his seed potatoes too deep.

4. This is one of the things they argue about.

5. The others are evolution, the Rolling Stones and the Labour Party.

6. My mum works in a hospice feeding people who are going to die.

7. She says it's not the same food we have at home.

8. Nan shouts at the wrestling on TV. Grandad lives mostly in the shed.

9. My twin sisters Lucy and Charlotte are both four years older than me.

10. They tell me I was an accident. Mum says if I was, no one was hurt.

My 10 Top Matchbox Cars

1. Mercedes-Benz – present from Uncle Fritz* to make up for World War II.

2. VW Fastback – same car as my dad's but in better condition.

3. Ford Zodiac with removable spare tyre which got lost immediately.

4. Rolls-Royce Silver Shadow – I only drive this on carpet.

5. Mercury Station Wagon – huge American car. Quite difficult to park.

6. Ford Cortina – borrowed from cousin Eric who has eight exactly the same.

7. Ford Transit camper van. I sometimes leave it out somewhere overnight.

8. Leyland lorry with joinable pipes for sewage projects (Dad's favourite).

9. Ford GT so fast it's very difficult to control especially on kitchen floor.

10. Caravan. Stays parked in lay-by to offer Hot and Cold Food.

* Not a real uncle. Actually a German POW who stayed with my grandparents after the war for about 10 years doing the washing-up.

What Happened to Paul Jenkins's Felt Tips

1. Paul Jenkins had twelve new felt tips in his brand-new pencil case.

2. Six felt tips went missing including the red one.

3. All the class had to look for them on the floor and in our pencil cases.

4. Michael Thompson found the six missing ones in his pencil case.

5. Including the red one. Mr Bennett said he was caught red-handed.

6. Mr Bennett then hit him on the hand with a ruler once for every felt tip.

7. At the end Michael Thompson's hand was even redder.

8. Paul Jenkins and Michael Thompson are no longer friends.

9. Although to be honest they weren't friends in the first place.

10. The mystery is why he only stole six. Maybe he thought that was fair.

Why My Dad Thinks My Nan Spoils Me

1. My nan is incredibly old. Dad is her youngest child and he's already old.

2. Nan remembers a Zeppelin coming down in the First World War.

3. A lot of the food she cooks has been picked or grown or hunted.

4. She once skinned a rabbit which we had to eat for lunch.

5. I didn't really like it but she doesn't take any nonsense.

6. She gives my grandad bread and dripping for his lunch.

7. Dripping is a layer of cold white fat on bread which is a treat for OAPs.*

8. Nan's larder is full of millions of jars of unidentified pickled stuff.

9. The only real food she ever has in the larder is Rice Krispies.

10. Which she makes for me with hot milk. Dad says this is 'unprecedented'.

* Grandad says he smeared goose fat on himself when he was a child to keep warm. I'm surprised someone didn't eat him for the dripping.

Best Things Me and Steve Baker Did on the Summer Holidays

1. Played cards with four packs at the same time. I had seven jokers.

2. Took specially selected Matchbox cars on jungle safari down garden.

3. Invented Subbuteo human sacrifice game. I lost whole team.

4. Built hay-bale fort and defended it against Germans until tea.

5. Rebuilt fort with cousin Eric with 'improvements' suggested by Dad.

6. Visited Eric with broken arm in hospital after fall from 'improvements'.

7. Took bus into town with Ruth Simons and Emma Standish.*

8. Slept in tent at bottom of garden with squash and digestive biscuits.

9. Sold Mum's quince pears to old ladies in street. Made 85p.

10. Sent to room for selling Mum's quince pears. Returned 55p.

* I invited Becky Hatton but the girls said they hated her.

What I Do When I'm Sent to My Room

1. Throw myself on bed, sniff and then sulk for a bit.

2. Listen hard for extra punishments being prepared downstairs.

3. Try sucking my thumb again but realise I'm far too grown up.

4. Remind myself once again of how fundamentally unfair life is.

5. Decide not to run away from home in case that involves camping.

6. Get my big box of Lego out and build something utterly brilliant.

7. So brilliant that it makes my parents look very small indeed.

8. With their made-up rules about stuff that is not important to anyone.

9. Line up my teddies as judging committee for Lego building competition.

10. Award myself prize. Ask if I can come down for tea.

The First Tragedy in My Life

1. It was bad for me but much worse for my pet rabbit Worthington.

2. I said I wanted a rabbit after reading *Watership Down*.

3. My dad spent about a month building a fox-proof hutch.

4. I think he used the plans for a nuclear bunker.

5. Last night a strange noise woke me up. It was Worthington screaming.

6. I looked out of the window and saw a badger attacking the hutch.

7. I went to get my dad but similar noises were coming from their bedroom.

8. I thought the whole house was being attacked by badgers.

9. This morning Worthington was still safe in his hutch but dead.

10. Of shock my dad said. Although him and Mum seemed to be OK.

My First Impressions of Big School

1. Everyone wears long trousers. I have said goodbye to my knees.

2. The big kids are massive. I suddenly feel small again.

3. We go to school on the bus. I sit on the top front seat.

4. Big kids sit at the back. Poor choice in my opinion.

5. Detention is really easy to get. I am learning harsh self-discipline.

6. Steve is in a different form. He already has detention.

7. There is a girl in my form called Hyacinth. Like the flower.

8. I said Hi to her. She says that is not her nickname.

9. I might be in love with Hyacinth. She is tall but not from distant Ophir.

10. We get homework which is unfair. But I already know how unfair life is.

Why I Don't Like Football

1. I can't get my foot to connect with the ball. Especially when it's moving.

2. When I try to kick it some other idiot gets in the way. Or takes it.

3. If the ball hits you it really hurts. Especially the head.

4. I don't understand what 'man on' means. What does it mean?

5. Wouldn't it be easier if everyone was on the same side?

6. I can run very fast but not with the ball.

7. I am best at 'getting into space' and staying there. Alone.

8. I don't trade football cards because I don't have any.

9. I don't support Chelsea or anyone. How do you get started with a team?

10. My parents have never even mentioned football. Didn't they notice it?

Weird Things My Mum Does with My Sandwiches*

1. Wraps them in Christmas napkins for first six months of year.

2. Cuts sandwiches in shape of a heart (I stopped this one immediately).

3. Uses apple corer to take middle out and make Japanese flag.

4. Gives me slightly stale mini Japanese suns the following day.

5. Encourages 'healthy grazing' by cutting sandwiches into sixteenths.

6. Sandwiches wrapped in 'Interesting' book reviews from newspaper.

7. Feudal agriculture days. Long thin strips of sandwiches.

8. Up to 20 layers of tinfoil/cling film for pass-the-parcel lunch.

9. Snippets of inspirational poetry put in box (normally about food).

10. Added instructions to make smiley face with tomatoes and carrot.

* I have school dinners now.

How My Mum and Dad Are Doing as Parents So Far

1. Food is generally delivered on time and usually hot.

2. There is far too much vegetables and not enough chips.

3. They have some kind of religious objection to fizzy drinks.

4. There are many cast-iron rules that suddenly emerge from nowhere.

5. My mother 'talks it out' with me for hours until I'm totally confused.

6. When my father points at me, danger is imminent.

7. My dad has punished me by whacking me with a slipper twice.

8. Apparently it hurts him more than me. He loves his slippers.

9. I have been promised £100 if I don't smoke before I'm 18.

10. Seeing them dance together is excruciating, embarrassing, sickening.

Why My Twin Sisters Lucy and Charlotte Totally Ignore Me

1. They are in self-contained twindom (not to be confused with Swindon).

2. I am a 'sullen, spotty, filthy, hormonal herbert'.

3. They know what each other is going to say before they even say it.

4. Nothing I could ever say would ever interest them ever.

5. I don't get girls' 'complex relationship dynamics' (what are they?).

6. I am only interested in 'banging things together'.

7. Science has proven that boys are always 15 years less mature than girls.

8. Everything I am doing now they have already done better and neater.

9. My school friends are all cretins.

10. They think I smell.

My Brutal New Hygiene Regime

1. I shower/bath every day whether I need to or not.

2. I use Zest soap because it makes me smell like lemon meringue pie.

3. My flannel is blue. It has the world's worst job.

4. I scrub really thoroughly under my arms because they are the pits.

5. Wash toes carefully. Nobody wants athlete's foot, especially not athletes.

6. I wash my bottom and my toggle and the strange area between.

7. My father calls this 'the mushroom danger area'.

8. He means a high danger of fungal growth. I no longer eat mushrooms.

9. I dry myself vigorously to 'prevent chapping' as my mother says.

10. Which I believe is some kind of saddle sore.

How Limestone Led Almost Directly to My First Kiss

1. My class went on a Geography field trip to Malton in Yorkshire.

2. We have reached the age where we all need to know about limestone.

3. Three other schools were also there because of the limestone.

4. On the final night there was a disco. I wore my new brown corduroys.

5. 'Knock on Wood' by Amii Stewart jump-started me onto the dance floor.

6. A new girl danced next to me which was exciting and frightening.

7. We did some pretty fancy moves and then I bought her a Coke.

8. Steve Baker was kissing her friend. We sat and watched for a moment.

9. I sensed something needed to be done. She pointed to her lips.

10. I aimed for them with mine. IT WAS LIKE THUNDER! LIGHTNING!*

    * Lyrics from 'Knock on Wood' by Amii Stewart.

Why Steve Baker and I Don't Seem to be Friends Any More

1. Steve is now cool. I don't even know how that works.

2. Steve is attractive to girls without making superhuman efforts.

3. Steve smokes. I need my lungs for running and the £100.

4. Steve doesn't run like he used to. He was a brilliant sprinter.

5. Steve sits at the back of the bus. I still prefer the front.

6. Steve doesn't work and is in the bottom set with the dummers.

7. Steve's parents are divorcing which makes him sad and interesting.

8. Steve listens to music that is basically angry shouting.

9. Steve thinks I'm a bit immature. Mum says I'm definitely not.

10. My parents say he's wasting his life. I might try wasting some of mine.

How My Sister Lucy Became a Total Adult Virtually Overnight

1. Lucy went out* and got her first job as a waitress in Aloha.

2. Aloha is a local Hawaiian-themed restaurant down by the station.

3. It's famous for its Full English Breakfasts. With pineapple.

4. The pineapple is the only thing that has anything to do with Hawaii.

5. Lucy doesn't have to wear a hula skirt or say 'aloha'.

6. At home she tells everyone she is on the PAYE scheme which she loves.

7. In her eyes the PAYE scheme makes her totally grown up.

8. She has actually written to the tax office to introduce herself.

9. And is now looking forward to doing her first annual tax return.

10. My parents are more worried about Lucy than I've ever seen them before.

    * She told Charlotte to wait at home.

How I Miraculously Acquired Some Cool Points

1. Grew to just over six foot tall. Might still be growing.

2. Forgot to brush hair and realised it looked better.

3. Increased the width of my tie knot to size of grapefruit.

4. Stopped wearing my coat and literally became a lot cooler.

5. Slowed my walk down so that other cool people could keep up with me.

6. Beat Karl Edwards (who everyone hates) in school cross-country.

7. Dumped Becky Hatton because she was three-timing me.*

8. Designed the stage set for *Romeo and Juliet* as a disco laundry.

9. I'm not an embarrassing dancer which everyone assumed I would be.

10. Ruth likes my music collection. I might have to take her to Funky Town.

* Steve Baker and Lance Adams. Don't think she realised you have to dump old boyfriends before getting new ones.

Highlights of Fifth Form School Trip to Normandy

1. Steve Baker bought panatella cigars in duty-free shop on ferry.

2. Smoked my first cigar (not a cigarette so £100 from parents safe).

3. Saw Bayeux Tapestry. How did we get invaded by needlepoint experts?

4. Steve got drunk on Calvados and scraped face down pebbledash wall.

5. Fell slightly in love with Sandrine our tall French tour guide.

6. Ruth thinks she is patronising. I think she is beautifully haughty.

7. Mixed feelings about Sandrine's armpit hair. Exotic or repulsive?

8. Mr Johnson our Geography teacher accused coach driver of drunk-driving.

9. Extra day in Dinard because of no coach. Smoked panatella.

10. What language exactly do the French speak? Nothing we've been taught.

Reasons That I Am Now Probably a Man

1. I know how to shave with a razor and can pull all the faces.

2. I was in the top third of finishers in Aylesbury 10k race. Impressive.

3. I haven't played with Lego for months. Not properly anyway.

4. I can see through the hypocrisy of grown-ups. They just don't get it.

5. I have driven a car (in Sainsbury's car park).

6. I now know what girls want even though I haven't got most of it.

7. My voice is deep and manly but sometimes doesn't stay down.

8. I have read Dostoevsky and empathise with the Russian *weltschmerz*.

9. I know what *weltschmerz* means. It means world-weariness.

10. I get very *weltschmerzy* when I think of the untouchable Emma Standish.

What I Think of My Sisters Now I'm a Lot Taller Than Them

1. Their self-contained world is smaller than I thought.

2. I'm not the only one excluded. Mum and Dad are too.

3. They don't like the outside world and are therefore rude about it.

4. Lucy subtly bullies Charlotte. Often without speaking.

5. Boys are quickly attracted to them and then slowly repulsed.

6. They never stop communicating even when they're silent.

7. They're like one brain in two bodies. With four feet.

8. I feel like the moon orbiting them. Dark and dead.

9. I don't think they'll ever change. They finished developing in the womb.

10. They are planning to move out to a small flat. I already don't miss them.

My Ingenious But Fattening Method of Revision

1. Obviously the first thing I do is write a list of 10 things to revise.

2. The first six things are the absolute minimum required to dispel ignorance.

3. Points 7 and 8 will probably get me 'solid passes'.*

4. Do 9 & 10 and I will cause the examiners ripples of excitement.

5. Points revised earn Maltesers. First point has one, second has two, etc.

6. This evening I have done an impressive 10-pointer revision session.

7. I've also eaten 55 Maltesers (2¾ bags).

8. Which makes me feel exceptionally well prepared but sick.

9. I'm going to have to come up with a new Malteser/revision algorithm.

10. But first I've got to look up exactly what algorithm means again.

    * What my dad calls them. Don't know why.

Head vs Heart vs Breasts

1. I think I should probably go out with Ruth Simons.

2. We listen to music together in her bedroom for hours.

3. She is Mum's best friend's daughter so it's kind of convenient.

4. But when I turn the light off at night I think of Becky Hatton.

5. Especially her breasts.

6. Technically I understand they are two bags of fat.

7. But they generate more heat in my body than a Bessemer blast furnace.

8. Ruth has given me *The Female Eunuch* by Germaine Greer* to read.

9. I think she's laying the groundwork for us going out.

10. The breasts on the cover remind me of Becky Hatton.

* Important Feminist Literature.

My O-Level Results with Notes

1. CHEMISTRY – A   Impressive reaction from teacher.

2. PHYSICS – A   Magic moment(s).

3. BIOLOGY – B   B is for Biology so that seems fair.

4. MATHS – A   It was my algorithms that did it.

5. ART – A   Not bad for glorified doodling.

6. FRENCH – D   Total waste of Maltesers.

7. GEOGRAPHY – B   Found glaciers a bit slow-moving.

8. HISTORY – C   Disappointing but it's all in the past now.

9. ENGLISH LANG. – A   Mother very happy.

10. ENGLISH LIT. – A   Mother almost weeping.

Things My Dad Says Which Make Absolutely No Sense At All

1. You can't take it with you but you can leave it with the concierge.

2. Bats don't see by radar. They hear by ASDIC (some navy thing).

3. Nymphs and shepherds come away, come away, come away (*sung*).

4. Spinach is edible girders (thought it was 'girdles' for a time).

5. Don't talk back, [followed by] What have you got to say for yourself?

6. When I'm reading the paper I am in a separate inaccessible dimension.

7. If you want something done ask an engineer. And he'll ask your mother.

8. We're not getting a second home until you appreciate the first one.

9. Supermarket car parks are the most dangerous places on earth.

10. You never know what you've got until you've checked the shed.

My First Out-of-Body Experience

1. My dad wants me to study three sciences for A level. Mum doesn't.

2. The Headmaster offered us all tea and biscuits including me.

3. Which was a reassuring sign that I wasn't about to be punished.

4. They then talked about me as if I was a piece of cheese.

5. The Head said that two sciences and English literature was unheard of.

6. But would lead to a well-rounded individual, countered my mum.

7. The Head teaches Chemistry so definitely wasn't impressed by that.

8. My dad then said what was needed was a 'polyvalent' solution.

9. Something happened to the Head's face which I think was a smile.

10. Afterwards my mum kissed my dad on the school premises.*

    * I almost went for three sciences at that point.

How I'm Preparing for My Date with Ruth Simons

1. Reminded myself that girls are also hominids and share much of our DNA.

2. Practised a three-second delay before speaking to eliminate crassness.

3. Skimmed through a book of the nation's favourite poems for added depth.

4. Shaved incredibly carefully round major blackhead-incident zone.

5. Selected clothes that are cool and haven't been knitted by Nan.

6. Developed knowing laugh for things she says I don't quite hear/get.

7. Packed handkerchief for nervous sweating or sudden nosebleed.

8. Loosened shoelaces to prevent me walking too fast and disappearing.

9. Ironed blue underpants then decided to go for relaxed white look.

10. Borrowed three condoms from Steve. Sale or return.

Post-Match Analysis of First Date with Ruth

1. No physical injuries, scrapes, sprains, lesions, scuff marks, etc.

2. Crassness delay failed on two occasions. Rapid backtracking required.

3. A lot of conversation was about Emma Standish and Lance Adams.

4. Long discussion about 'what's going on' between Emma and Lance.

5. Unsuccessfully attempted to divert conversation towards music charts.

6. Unexplained sudden weeping (Ruth). Nothing to do with me apparently.

7. Tried empathisation. Deployed handkerchief. Declined.

8. Walked home together. Attempted light *Female Eunuch*-based chat.

9. Hug from Ruth. Breasts held clear. Hair in face. Awkward.

10. Kept Steve's condoms in case I've totally misread situation.

How the World Looks Now That I Have Finally Had Sex*

1. I now sit at the back of the bus through sheer weight of *weltschmerz*.

2. The world has nothing left to teach me. I've reached its wildest shores.

3. I won't be reading poetry any more. Kind of misses the point.

4. Feel my appearance has changed outwardly but don't quite know how.

5. I didn't expect sex involving me could be that good.

6. Love and sex aren't the same thing. Not sure which one feels better.

7. There is no part of a girl which isn't supercharged with electricity.

8. I don't want to have children with Becky Hatton. I'm just not ready.

9. But using a condom is like having a clown present during sex.

10. Relieved that my running times haven't been adversely affected.

   * With Becky Hatton. Not exactly what I was planning but 'life is about changes and how you respond to them' (according to Dad).

How a Morris Marina Nearly Got Between My Twin Sisters

1. Lucy seems to have no trouble attracting male attention.

2. Most of this she treats with the absolute contempt it deserves.

3. But Barry has passed his test and has a Morris Marina Coupé.

4. Everyone knows that this is the wankiest car in history.

5. Barry is happy to drive Lucy around town. Which she likes.

6. They visit shops and other places of interest.

7. Then Charlotte asked Barry for a lift into town. Barry said yes.

8. He doesn't know that twins look similar but are subtly different.

9. Like the Morris Marina 1.3 and 1.8. Same chassis, different engine.

10. Barry was dumped immediately so now there's no lifts for anyone.

What Happens Now That I Am Officially Going Out with Ruth*

1. I cycle across to her house with my cycle clips on.

2. For coolness I make absolutely sure that I take my cycle clips off.

3. Her mum asks whether I want to stay for supper.

4. I say no because I've already had tea at home

5. Wonder again what the difference between tea and supper is.

6. Also the Simonses eat a lot of weird pasta which I don't like.

7. Unless it's Spaghetti Bolognese which isn't really pasta.

8. Go up to Ruth's room and listen to Diana Ross/Donna Summer.**

9. We snog a bit but Ruth always ruins it by talking.

10. We have both agreed not to have sex until we're married.

* Our first date was a success I discovered afterwards.

** Not much Donna Summer because apparently it excites me too much.

Why My Eighteenth Birthday Wasn't as Good as I Was Hoping

1. I said I wanted a party for all my friends with a hog roast.

2. My dad went out and bought the pig.

3. Which might as well have been a guinea pig. It was a piglet.

4. Dad said it would feed all my friends which implied I didn't have many.

5. Some of the girls were horrified by the poor little piglet on the spit.

6. My dad tried to cook it on a bonfire which just singed it.

7. In the end Dad poured petrol on the pig and cremated it.

8. Steve Baker drank most of the cider and then vomited in the compost.

9. We left for the pub because I was too embarrassed to stay at home.

10. My parents claimed my £100 no-smoking money in damages.*

    * They gave it to me after I threatened to start smoking.

'Solid Reasons' My Father Has Not to Study English at University*

1. You won't be able to read a book for pleasure ever again.

2. You won't help British manufacturing compete with Germany/Japan.

3. There's a genuine danger of slipping into amateur dramatics.

4. All English teachers are Marxists bent on revolution.

5. The other people on your course will be intellectuals/sexual deviants.

6. You don't study decent authors like Wilbur Smith.

7. It's not an academic discipline like Science where you have to know stuff.

8. If books really are your thing you can read on the train.

9. You will be completely unemployable except as a Marxist English teacher.

10. Your cousin Eric studied English and now he's in some kind of asylum.

* Rerun of A-level debate. 'Polyvalent' solution only possible in USA.

'Passionate Pleas' from My Mother on Why I *Should* Study English

1. Eric is actually a civil servant and doing really well.

2. All that's worth knowing about life is in the pages of great literature.

3. You'll have plenty of time to develop other interests like drama.

4. Only the most sensitive and intuitive people are drawn to literature.

5. That's why your father studied engineering and now works underground.

6. By deconstructing great books you can discover the politics behind them.

7. Scientists can be rather dull and laboratories often smell quite odd.

8. Rats shouldn't be dissected. Which is what most scientists do.

9. Your consciousness is less likely to evolve if you study Sciences.

10. Your mother studied English and it was the happiest time of her life.

Why I am Going to Study Engineering at University

1. My father makes a lot of sense. He has done well underground.

2. My mother studied English and is prone to weeping over nothing.

3. Engineering is a very useful subject and I will get a good job.

4. I worked really hard to get Science A levels. Why waste them?

5. Engineers get to work on big important projects of national significance.

6. When I look at myself in the mirror I see engineer. Civil engineer.

7. Ruth chucked me.

8. If she's the kind of person studying English then count me out.

9. To be honest, there's a whiff of self-indulgence about literature.

10. What would you rather have? Philip Larkin or mains drainage?

How My Relationship with Ruth Ended

1. I suggested that we should go to a comedy club in London.

2. She said she didn't want to plan too far ahead.

3. Is two days 'too far ahead'? I asked somewhat surprised.

4. She felt we didn't want the same things and she needed space to grow.

5. I said, 'You're a bit young for an allotment.'

6. Me not taking serious things seriously was another reason for us splitting.

7. How many other reasons were there? I stopped her at six.

8. Was there someone else involved? Lance Adams for example.

9. He's really sweet but he's just a friend.

10. In a holding pattern with his undercarriage down. Goodbye.

Technical Reasons Why I Failed My Driving Test

1. Driving off without examiner.

2. Not getting into right lane to turn right off one-way street.

3. Noticing Ruth out with Lance walking hand in hand.

4. If she wants to go out with someone that shallow then fine.

5. It's incredibly unlikely that he'll become a professional footballer.

6. And what about your famous love of poetry and literature?

7. And feelings! Do you think Lance has any of those? I think not.

8. You never dressed like that when we went out. Utter hypocrisy.

9. In terms of boyfriends you're now on a downward slope, Ruth.

10. Failing to stop for pedestrian on zebra crossing.

My First Day at University and Possibly My Last Day at Home Ever

1. My mum and dad were supposed to take me and my stuff to university.

2. The car was absolutely packed then my mum carried a box of books out.

3. She said it was a selection of literature important for 'balance'.

4. Then they had a row. A big one.

5. It started with books then escalated to arts vs sciences.

6. I knew the next level was politics so I went inside.

7. Dad ended up driving me. The first hour was in total silence.

8. He did a lot of aggressive overtaking and swearing.

9. We found my room and unloaded. He apologised, gave me £40 and left.

10. I got my Earth, Wind & Fire poster up and faced my future alone.

New Stuff I Have Learned as a Student (Excluding Engineering)

1. Lecturers can't lecture. They shouldn't even be allowed to.

2. Laundry is a never-ending cripplingly expensive industrial process.

3. I have investigated sending my laundry home by post.

4. It's easy to make new friends. Tom, Ben and Ronnie.

5. It's very difficult to get rid of your new friends, Ben and Ronnie.

6. Beer makes you feel very studenty and mature and involved.

7. I literally cannot talk at breakfast. I struggle to get things in my mouth.

8. The library has an impenetrable force field. I simply bounce off it.

9. Athletics is incredibly competitive. Do they have an extra lung?

10. I'm the first engineering student ever to audition for *Waiting for Godot*.*

   * Haven't heard anything yet.

Why Breakfast is the Low Point of My Day

1. The toaster in the dining hall is an engineering slap in the face.

2. You place two slices of bread on a little conveyor belt.

3. After about five minutes they finally disappear into the toaster.

4. You then have enough time to get yourself a coffee.

5. Later that morning the toast drops out of the other end.

6. Still completely white but slightly less bendy.

7. Then some criminal takes them because he's been waiting half an hour.

8. Your two slices are still in there somewhere doing absolutely nothing.

9. When I graduate I'm going to completely redesign the toaster.

10. And the computer, the phone, the watch and the Hoover.

How My New Friend Tom Raised My Sophistication Levels

1. I was at the back gate of college warming up for a run.

2. Someone I recognised from the toast machine joined me in his kit.

3. He asked to run with me. I suddenly felt I was in *Chariots of Fire*.

4. We started running and chatting for a few miles.

5. He stopped chatting. I said are you OK? He said, 'Couldn't be better.'

6. Then he threw up. I think I recognised my toast.

7. We walked back slowly. He was studying philosophy.

8. Philosophy was 'invisible engineering'. So completely useless, I said.*

9. He asked about classical music. I said 'Knock on Wood' was a classic.

10. That evening he made a mix tape just for me called 'Emergency Culture'.

    * He agreed. That's when I knew he was all right.

Why You Should Never Mix Sex and Culture

1. Amazingly I got the part of Taurus in *Antony and Cleopatra*.

2. Taurus says, 'My Lord?'* I've tried the line about 300 different ways.

3. In the play I have to lead an army across the stage. Without speaking.

4. During the wait I chatted to Charmian.** We snogged (in character).

5. Later we had a drink. She came up to my room. Sex looked unavoidable.

6. To enhance the mood I put 'Emergency Culture' on my ghetto blaster.

7. The first track was 'Ride of the Valkyries'. Foreplay got a bit heated.

8. The next track was 'The Minute Waltz'. Last thing I needed.

9. Beethoven's 'Ode to Joy' was next. Charmian turned it off just in time.

10. I put on the Pointer Sisters. 'Slow Hand' came on and we started again.

* It's the only thing he says.
** Cleopatra's handmaiden.

Why You Should Also Never Mix Sport and Culture

1. I tried to get selected for the uni athletics team for the nationals.

2. But didn't make the grade in any event. I'm just not fast enough.

3. Our captain Dan said no one had tried out for the 10k walk.

4. That's because it looks ridiculous I told him. He said I'd get a club tie.

5. I practised a bit of speed walking. Alone in my room obviously.

6. Went to Crystal Palace. Walked 10k looking like a twat. Came last.

7. Had great club dinner. I got special award for 'Entertainment'.

8. Got out of bed backwards because hamstrings were now length of Chile.

9. Couldn't lead the army across the stage for *Antony and Cleopatra*.

10. My mate Tom had to come on and point the army in the right direction.

My 'Date' with Emma Standish

1. During the vacation I had a call from Leon, an old friend from school.

2. Leon said he was going to the Dealers gig in town, Steve Baker's band.

3. They're a kind of New Wave punk band quite big on the local scene.

4. I said it wasn't my kind of music. He said that Emma Standish was going.

5. And apparently she had said It would be good to see me.

6. The gig was in the back room of a pub. The speakers filled half the room.

7. A big picture of Edvard Munch's *The Scream* was their backdrop.

8. Steve looked and sang like the screaming man in the painting.

9. Emma danced in front of Steve all night. I really hated him and his music.

10. Outside I put The Temptations* on my Walkman like emergency oxygen.

* 'Papa Was a Rollin' Stone'.

Contents of My Food Parcel from Nan in Order of Usefulness

1. Brand-new five-pound note (probably specially ordered from bank).

2. Variety pack of cereals including Rice Krispies.

3. Home-made gingerbread in greaseproof paper.

4. Miniature of Drambuie. Good for colds apparently.

5. Cuttings from local newspaper about engineering jobs.

6. Free 1983 Calendar from Liddle Johnson Solicitors.

7. Green bobble hat knitted from world's roughest wool.

8. Handwritten letter keeping me up to date with her garden.

9. Plum jam.

10. Cuttings about my 'friend' Alex Cartwright also doing well at college.

Things I Learned About Myself at Student Dinner Party

1. Everything I say is framed in patriarchal language and is thus invalid.

2. I am complicit in the subjugation of all women.

3. I am a rapist. Or at the very least a potential one.

4. Engineering is a male construct designed to perpetuate patriarchy.

5. I have oppressed virtually any culture you care to mention.

6. I am a victim of my own belief system and can't see it.

7. I am an evolutionary cul-de-sac along with the Neanderthals.

8. I have personal responsibility for the slave trade (African not Roman).

9. I am a homophone (I think that's what they said).

10. I don't really like fondue.

How Alex Cartwright Unremembered Our Primary School

1. I saw him at an athletics club party. He looked exactly the same: smooth.

2. He was very busy working his way round the room chatting and smiling.

3. He finally got to me. It took him a minute before he recognised me.

4. And then he faltered briefly as if he'd been caught out.

5. He seemed to have moved up several social classes since primary school.*

6. His clothing had also taken a different and more expensive route to mine.

7. Gamekeeper or some kind of rural hunting thing seemed to be the theme.

8. He wasn't at all keen to reminisce about primary school.

9. He pretended not to remember Emma Standish. Which is impossible.

10. Maybe he had some kind of personal Year Zero and erased everything.

* Afterwards he went away to a boarding school somewhere.

How I Got Serious about My Exams on Platform 2 at 4am

1. During the Christmas hols I worked nights at the Mail Sorting Office.

2. All us students were sorting mail into little slots for delivery.

3. I was picked by an old bloke called Bill to help him out with something.

4. I don't know why he chose me although I did pass him the sugar earlier.

5. We collected sacks of sorted mail and drove them to the station.

6. We waited for the mail train in the rain and then threw the sacks inside.

7. We then drank whisky in the stationmaster's toasty office.

8. They took the piss for an hour or so about me being a posh student.

9. Then we fetched more wet mail sacks and threw them on the next train.

10. Bill's done it for 34 years. He told me to bugger off and pass my exams.

My First Slightly Disappointing Brush with the Occult

1. I took a beautiful girl called Lorraine to our midsummer ball.

2. I was pretty much completely in love with her by 8.30pm.

3. She encouraged me to have my Tarot cards read in a little booth.

4. The lady inside looked more like a legal secretary than a soothsayer.

5. She read my cards as if my destiny were instructions on a can of soup.

6. The Fool overlaying the Emperor said I was entertaining but competent.

7. The Page of Cups showed that I was impetuous in matters of the heart.

8. Then there was a nasty-looking card of a tower being hit by lightning.

9. Probably the occupational hazards of electrical engineering, I explained.

10. She said it would mean tragedy in my life but that all would be well.

How These Predictions Came True Sooner Than I Anticipated

1. Before I left the booth I was given a cassette tape of the reading.

2. Outside there was no sign of Lorraine anywhere.

3. I looked for her everywhere for about two hours. She'd disappeared.

4. Then someone told me she'd gone off with some other bloke.

5. Which in its way was a bit of a tragedy.

6. But then I remembered that all would be well.

7. It was only 11.28 and knowing me I could be deeply in love by midnight.

8. And that was pretty much what happened with Deborah.

9. As an added bonus she was also beautifully tall.

10. Which means she could have been the tower hit by lightning. Spooky!

How It Felt After I Finished My Final Exams

1. After I'd recovered from my hangover I felt confused.

2. We had two weeks left in college with nothing to do.

3. I think I went slightly mad. I felt as if my youth had suddenly finished.

4. The libraries didn't care if I went in or not. I felt rejected.

5. There was nothing left between me and the outside world.

6. Unless I took another degree. And got really really educated.

7. But you can't do that forever unless you're going to grow a beard.

8. Instead I got off with Michelle Ayers. Who I didn't even know I fancied.

9. It felt like a *weltschmerzy, fin de siècle, götterdämmerung* kind of thing.

10. And then it was all over. And I had a tasselled hat.

My Last Holiday Before Maturity and Responsibility

1. Tom and I decided to go to Paris for the summer to improve our French.

2. We stayed in a tiny flat six floors up just off the Rue Mogador.

3. On the first night I looked out of the window across the inner courtyard.

4. In the kitchen below a beautiful girl was peeling potatoes half naked.

5. We admired her potato-peeling technique for some time.

6. Then we heard her speaking English to someone else indoors.

7. The following day we made contact. Their names were Helen and Jane.

8. They worked in Marks & Spencer just round the corner on Bvd Haussmann.

9. Jane moved upstairs with Tom, I migrated downstairs to Helen.

10. That's why I have very fond memories of Paris but can't speak French.

Reasons I'm Worrying About My First Engineering Job Interview

1. I've put my brand-new suit on and now feel like a pantomime horse.

2. My tie chokes me to death. I can hardly breathe let alone speak.

3. The interviewing panel already hate me and have shredded my CV.

4. I can't take myself seriously so why should they? No reason.

5. Why would anybody pay me money to mess things up? They wouldn't.

6. There are billions of better-looking, better-qualified people out there.

7. With winning smiles, sparkling anecdotes and powerful connections.

8. Being a waiter is fine by me. No honestly. I'm a people person.

9. That's the kind of rubbish I'll be saying in the interview.

10. Before I inadvertently call the chairman 'Dad'.

What Actually Happened in My First Engineering Job Interview

1. On the way in I banged my funny bone quite hard on the door frame.

2. I made a kind of screechy howl which I tried to make sound professional.

3. It really, really hurt and I may have used the F-word. Repeatedly.

4. The panel started laughing and asked if I was all right.

5. I said my arm was now completely numb and I rubbed it like Aladdin.

6. Mr Big Cheese said it was the best entrance they'd had all morning.

7. I said, 'Wait until you see my exit.'

8. Expected to be shown the door right then but was beyond caring.

9. They asked me if I was OK to answer a few questions.

10. I said, 'Yes, but be gentle.' And they were. Wimps.

Charlotte Raises the Stakes in the Crap Boyfriend Challenge

1. When men meet the twins they always seem to talk to Lucy first.

2. She doesn't say anything but it's like she's the gatekeeper.

3. Nigel talked to Charlotte first which got him big brownie points.

4. Nigel has an incredibly expensive Rolex watch which he often mentions.

5. It's so expensive that he doesn't ever wear it in case it's nicked.

6. But the very expensive Rolex needs movement to keep it wound up.

7. So he takes the Rolex for a walk every Sunday. Like a dog.

8. Charlotte secretly thinks Nigel is a nob. But he's her nob.

9. Then he took her out for Sunday lunch. After they'd walked the watch.

10. But he didn't pay for her. Which meant his time was up.

My Boss Ron. Not Necessarily What I Expected

1. Before I entered the world of work I thought it would be tough.

2. I thought professionals would act professionally.

3. And I thought business people would be businesslike.

4. My new boss Ron is helping me with these misconceptions.

5. He admits that part of his brain is missing thanks to an early LSD habit.

6. He struggles to use his computer. He doesn't understand cut and paste.

7. He stores his secret files in the Wastepaper Bin on his computer.*

8. He adds up things on his spreadsheet with a calculator.

9. But he knows electrical engineering stuff that's not in any textbook.

10. He has an iced bun every day and moans with pleasure. I like him.

    * Which we found out when I kindly emptied it for him one day.

Well-Meaning and Timely Financial Advice to Myself

1. Stop spending immediately. You are now up to your neck in debt.

2. But you do have a one-bedroom flat to stay in and watch TV.

3. Instead of going out. Which you can't afford now. Or ever again.

4. Clothing is not important. Modify opinion of Nan's knitted tops

5. Stop eating. Findus Crispy Pancakes are an unnecessary luxury.

6. Soup is wholesome and nutritious and goes well with bread.

7. Which can be transformed into toast if you know how. Which I do.

8. Stay late at work to get pay rise and keep heating off at home.

9. Join local running club for fitness/warmth/social life.

10. Use phone, gas, water, boiler, Crispy Pancakes only in emergency.

How I Fell in Love with Two Voices on the Same Evening

1. I went to a party with no engineers, so the fun sort.

2. Heard something truly wonderful playing on the stereo.

3. Turned to the girl next to me to see if she knew what it was.

4. She whispered it was Ella Fitzgerald. Couldn't believe my ears.

5. She had the poshest voice I've ever heard. Like a desert zephyr.*

6. Her skin was like the porcelain my nan keeps behind glass.

7. Julia was studying art restoration and looked like the finished product.

8. When I started to talk she shushed me and told me to listen to Ella.

9. It was 'A Foggy Day in London Town'. Julia smiled at me.

10. I smiled back. The song finished and I felt we were already intimate.

* Warm gentle wind from the west NOT the large Ford saloon favoured by police forces in the sixties.

I Know How Early Unsuccessful Aviation Pioneers Must Have Felt

1. I asked posh Julia out for dinner. Mainly to listen to her voice.

2. Even before we ordered I was ready to fall in love from a great height.

3. I foolishly chose spaghetti. Impossible to eat and look sophisticated.

4. I turned my charm boosters to STUN and they seemed to be working.

5. We were having a wonderful time until she said she was engaged.

6. He was the heir to a massive family business with an agressive side parting.

7. She didn't seem terribly happy. Maybe it was an arranged marriage.

8. Later on, kissing her seemed to be definitely on the cards but I didn't.

9. Out of respect for the massive family business and side parting.

10. And because I'm a complete flaming idiot.

Forensic Examination of Why I Always Overpurchase Fairy Liquid

1. I have just bought a large bottle of Fairy Liquid.

2. I put it on the shelf in the cupboard under the sink where it belongs.

3. Along with the other four unopened large bottles of Fairy Liquid.

4. The bottle of Fairy Liquid I am currently using is half full.

5. As far as I am aware there is no imminent shortage of Fairy Liquid.

6. Every time I pass it in the supermarket I put Fairy Liquid in my trolley.

7. A psychotherapist would say that 'the trolley' represents my mind.

8. And the Fairy Liquid is a subconscious way of cleansing my conscience.

9. Which is one of the many reasons why I don't have a psychotherapist.

10. I think I just like the bottle. And Liquid Fairies.

Ten Reasons I Love Running

1. I am rubbish at every other sport except croquet and punting.

2. And they're probably not even sports.

3. I'm useless at darts, snooker, football, rugby, cricket, ice skating, etc.

4. I am built for running. Fairly tall, long legs, mildly antisocial.

5. Running doesn't hurt. I can run long distances in relative comfort.

6. As long as my hands are warm. Otherwise my legs don't work.

7. When I'm running my brain empties apart from my split times.

8. Other runners always say hello. Unlike cyclists who all look miserable.

9. Afterwards I feel that actually the world is all right for a moment.

10. I am successfully avoiding moral turpitude, morbid obesity and football.

The First Human Death in My Family

1. My grandad said he was feeling slightly unwell.

2. He left the room, sat down quietly and died.

3. No trouble to anyone. But then he never had been.

4. My dad said Grandad's handwritten will was a thing of beauty.

5. Everything was planned, right down to disposal of old paint in the shed.*

6. He had very bad TB in 1952 and had been preparing for death ever since.

7. The funeral was all paid for, hymns were chosen, wake venues listed.**

8. Grandad selected a small completely plain headstone with only his name.

9. He wanted everything nicely tidied up so he could get out of the way.

10. I think he might have been trying to get out of the way since 1952.

* Fill half-empty tins with sand/cat litter and take to tip.

** Different capacities depending on how popular he was at death.

Best Things About Being an Electrical Engineer

1. You are incredibly powerful. I can make a whole town go dark.*

2. Electrical engineers literally turn people on.

3. Their kettles mostly but probably in a lot of other subtle ways.

4. I can point out the cabinet that contains the controller for traffic lights.

5. You are working with invisible stuff that no one understands.

6. Which makes you pretty close to a magician. Without the pointy hat.

7. Nothing works without us unless you include ploughing with oxen.

8. You get sent to amazing places you would never dream of visiting.

9. You get incredible satisfaction from lighting up people's lives.

10. Sometimes a complex circuit board can move me to tears. Kidding!!

* Cirencester. Not my finest hour.

My First Wedding as an Independent Adult

1. I was invited to the wedding of Ruth May Simons and Lance Mark Adams.

2. I went along to show that I'd completely forgotten she chucked me.

3. And because I thought Emma Standish might be there.

4. Lance's best man was the tallest bloke I've met. Absolutely enormous.

5. He made the happy couple look like figures on a wedding cake.

6. His speech was a list of people, animals and things Lance had shagged.

7. Which made it seem that Ruth was all that was left unshagged.

8. Ruth's speech was brilliant but Lance was virtually unconscious by then.

9. Emma Standish was abroad, lighting up some distant part of the world.

10. I was so disappointed I ended up sleeping with Becky Hatton again.*

   * She is the first and seventh woman I have slept with.

A List of My Top 10 Blessings Now That I Am 25

1. I am relatively healthy apart from a dodgy cruciate ligament.

2. I am moderately attractive to certain women in low-lighting conditions.

3. I have loving and supportive parents (and sisters I suppose).

4. I have a good job with good prospects and I like Ron my boss.

5. I own 31% of a comfortable flat with soundproofing issues.

6. I never go hungry. Peckish is the worst I have to deal with.

7. I'm not persecuted for my beliefs. Possibly because I don't have any.

8. I have freedom of speech which I choose not to exercise mostly.

9. I live in a country with great institutions like the NHS and WHSmith.

10. I don't have to fight in a foreign war and be needlessly killed.

How My Training Is Going for the London Marathon

1. Huge bowl of porridge for breakfast. Slow release of energy.

2. Get to office early. Do all meaningful work before meetings start.

3. Make myself cup of coffee with three sugars. Chat to lovely PA Andrea.

4. Walk to my desk via IT to avoid Ron asking me out for lunchtime drink.

5. Run at lunch break. Shower without singing which feels unnatural.

6. Check sponsorship form to see if I've broken the £100 mark (nope).

7. Eat sandwiches at desk at two o'clock. Feel mighty good about myself.

8. Have vital meeting with myself at 3pm facing window so I can close eyes.

9. Check meeting rooms for leftover biscuits I can eat. Finish up work.

10. Go home. Lie in bath. Think deeply unprofessional thoughts about Andrea.

What My Bank Statement is Telling Me About Myself

1. My car insurance seems to go up every time I start the engine.

2. Filling with petrol is the most expensive five minutes of my month.

3. I've worked out that I spend more on pizza than electricity.

4. Which has given me a whole new perspective on my day job.

5. In fact I seem to spend more on pizza than I do on normal food.

6. If I gave up pizza I could pay off my mortgage five years earlier.

7. Per month, extra pizza toppings cost roughly the same as my phone bill.

8. I'm going to have to review the importance of pepperoni in my life.

9. Or communication.

10. Clothing accounts for remarkably little. It may be time for new pants.

Why Shared Showers Are Not Like They Appear in the Movies

1. Once you're both in you can hardly move.

2. You can't agree on a comfortable temperature.

3. One person's wet, the other person's dry.

4. You have to be double-jointed to reach the soap.

5. You get sad hippy hair within seconds.

6. The shower door is continually barged open.

7. You bang your collarbone on the soap dish.

8. If you drop something it's gone forever.

9. You're too close to see Andrea's beautiful body.

10. Sexual stuff is difficult and dangerous. But extremely clean.

The Most Frightened and Powerful and Relieved I've Ever Felt*

1. Ron told me there was an urgent job in the Caribbean. Excellent.

2. A supertanker was stranded in Curaçao. Completely powerless. Fine.

3. I had to fly out there and fix it. By myself. Immediately. Gulp.

4. I rang someone who knows all about ship electrics and why they go pop

5. He gave me something fat to read on the plane. With pictures.

6. Their Chief Engineer said 'thank God you're here' and rushed me below.

7. The generator room was hotter than a bath you wouldn't get into.

8. Opened the big metal box marked 'Do Not Open'. Saw fault right away.

9. Felt huge waves of relief. Prodded other random stuff and sucked teeth.

10. Pointed out fault, ordered part, shook hands, lay on beach, went home.

* Aside from losing my virginity to Becky Hatton.

Why I Don't Like Ron's Boss and Neither Does Ron

1. Ron's boss looks like Henry VIII, with a fat neck and a ginger beard.

2. He stands with his feet apart and his codpiece thrust forward.

3. He gets through a lot of Personal Assistants.

4. He is very keen on budgets, KPIs,* project reporting and big wins.

5. 90% of what he says is some kind of management jargon.

6. He is happiest when he is pushing the envelope out of the box.

7. But I don't think he could wire a plug without blowing himself up.

8. He was brought in specifically to manage Ron. But Ron is unmanageable.

9. They have long meetings behind glass where he circles Ron shouting.

10. Ron looks completely unconcerned as if he's watching TV.

* An advanced form of peanut, I believe.

My Cousin Bella's Amazing Wedding

1. My cousin Bella is a wild-child free spirit with a large Mohican.

2. Confusingly she also has the most perfect peaches and cream complexion.

3. She married Torc, a tattoo artist and biker and all-round lovely guy.

4. Bella got married in her mum's white dress with knee-high Doc Martens.

5. Torc was in a Teddy boy suit with only the tats on his face visible.

6. They left the church on a massive chopper and sidecar with 30 bikers.

7. The reception was in a field with the catering done by the Brownies.*

8. We had sandwiches on paper plates and fairy cakes with tea.

9. It was agreed that things would turn ugly at 8pm when the Brownies left.

10. My mum and dad left shortly before the Brownies.

* My Aunt Pat is the Great White Barn Owl** of the local Brownies.

** Very high-ranking Brownie rank equivalent to Squadron Leader in RAF.

My First Visit to the Eastern Bloc

1. My friend Tom got himself an acting job in Prague in a low-budget film.

2. He plays an inept policeman who is forever spilling his coffee.

3. That's where studying philosophy gets you, I told him.

4. He was quite philosophical about it.

5. Maybe because he has the most beautiful Czech girlfriend I've ever seen.

6. Tom says she's a little bit volatile and often tries to stab him.

7. I warned him once about dating women who are too highly strung.*

8. Czech women generally are friendly and independent and gorgeous.

9. They also seem to have a refreshing respect for electrical engineers.

10. I drank a lot of beer, ate a lot of cabbage and decided to move to Prague.

* He ignored me. His next girlfriend was a totally unhinged concert violinist.

How I Instantly Changed My Mind About Moving to Prague

1. I met Sabah at a Heathrow baggage carousel. She had beautiful luggage.

2. She is a cross between Sophia Loren and Queen Nefertiti.

3. She is training to be a gynaecologist and is insanely bright.

4. She has the deepest brown eyes of unfathomable beauty.

5. When she laughs you feel you have been given a priceless gift.

6. She comes from a completely alien and mysterious Middle Eastern culture.

7. She has the longest finest fingers. Her nails are like polished acorns.

8. The thought of them on any part of me gives me the screaming abdabs.

9. I have nearly crashed my car three times from sheer excitement.

10. I'm not sure Englishmen are built for this kind of passion. But here goes.

As Far As I Know What Happened to Sabah

1. Her father discovered she was seeing an English electrical engineer.

2. He flew over to London and took her back to Cairo.

3. She won't be finishing her studies. Not in London anyway.

4. I believe she is now engaged to an Egyptian army officer.

5. My letters to her have been sent back unopened.

6. The photos of us have also been returned. With her cut out.

7. Her flatmate said she sobbed uncontrollably when she left.

8. It is the only thing I cling on to. She didn't want to go.

9. I thought about going to Cairo. But my will is broken.

10. There will be no tall lady from distant Ophir. Not for me.

My Iron-Willed Strategy to Get Over Sabah

1. For a start I won't be writing any more lists. That's got to stop.

2. I will write a very lengthy novel about doomed cross-cultural love.

3. I will run until exhaustion shuts down my mental faculties.

4. I will have mindless physical encounters with shorter women.

5. Failing that I will seek spiritual solace in my Rubik's cube.

6. I will devote three years to cracking it. I will think of that alone.

7. I will make sure I don't look at books about Tutankhamun or Egypt.

8. I won't eat dates so that the Egyptian economy is paralysed.

9. My bitter cynicism will make *weltschmerz* look like mild indigestion.

10. I will get myself posted to a remote job in the far north.

My First Near-Death Experience

1. Sakhalin is a Russian island off the coast of Japan. Bizarre but true.

2. The Russians really hoped the island had lots of natural gas.

3. It doesn't have much else to recommend it. I know because I went there.

4. They had an offshore drilling rig. I had to make sure the power worked

5. We ate stew and drank vodka. It's the only way to keep the stew down.

6. The drill operator gets a bonus for every 100ft of continuous drilling.

7. When the rig drill was 5,000ft down I accidentally turned the power off.

8. He wanted to do to me what the Russians did to the Germans in 1945.

9. I said it was Health and Safety. Sadly there's no Russian translation.

10. To keep me alive I paid his bonus. It was the stew that nearly killed me.

Things I Missed in the Five Months I Was Going Out with Sabah

1. My mother wasn't well. I didn't speak to my parents once.

2. My running almost stopped. My times were rubbish.

3. I didn't see any of my friends. I made pathetic excuses.

4. At work I missed out on a beautiful job in South Africa.

5. Which would have done my career no end of favours.

6. I think I stopped eating. I certainly don't remember eating.

7. In fact I think I was actually completely off my chump.

8. A bad case of lovesickness. I'll have to watch that in future.

9. I suspect my internal wiring might be slightly faulty.

10. Sudden emotional power surges which can lead to dangerous blackouts.

What I Learned about My Mother's Mystery Illness

1. My dad called to say that my mother had gone into hospital.

2. He couldn't explain exactly why even after extensive grilling by me.

3. The closest we got was unspecified 'women's problems'.

4. Dad lowered his voice when he said this.

5. 'The sort of thing that got you burnt as a witch in the Middle Ages.'

6. From this I deduced that it was unlikely to be a broken leg.

7. No man of my father's generation has ever said 'menopause'.

8. Not out loud anyway. And certainly not in the company of ladies.

9. I visited with a bunch of flowers and a box of chocolate ginger.

10. Which is a lot better than a ducking stool.

Complications Arising From My Mother's Illness

1. My mother was in hospital for just under a week.

2. The twins Lucy and Charlotte didn't visit once.

3. Even though the 74 bus virtually goes from door to door.

4. Mum was incandescent with rage.

5. My dad whispered that intermittent incandescence was part of the illness.

6. Between incandescences I talked to Mum about the twins.

7. Apparently she's always felt excluded by the twins' self-sufficiency.

8. She misses the close mother–daughter bond some women have.

9. I didn't know whether this unusual candour was also part of the illness.

10. So I left most of the talking to my mum and the chocolate ginger.

How I Try to Make My Diet Seem More Sophisticated Than It Is

1. Delice de eggs on toast.

2. An loli of Rav served on a plated plate.

3. Toast à la toast.

4. Three Weetabix in a whole-milk jus. Partouffed with sugar.

5. Steak pie ennestled behind a beaver dam of chips.

6. Choppy wavelets of meringue in a golden bay of lemon pie.

7. Abignale of sausage, beans and chips with a pan-fried egg.

8. Chocolate Nobs of Hob.

9. Pied Cottage.

10. Demihemispheres of appled apple.

How Filling Up at Esso Prompted Recollections of my Collections

1. I started with stickers for the 1972 Munich Olympics from Esso.

2. Then miniature plaster heads of footballers in the 1974 World Cup.

3. I moved on to PG Tips cards. These are worth well into two figures now.

4. When I got the bus to school I collected bus numbers.

5. Which is why I had to sit at the front. I've never done train numbers.

6. I collected horse manure from a local park for my mum's roses.

7. That wasn't a permanent collection.

8. For a while I collected coins. Until I discovered that they were money.

9. I had Airfix models hanging from my ceiling. Except the ships obviously.

10. Now I collect air miles, John Lee Hooker albums and scars on my heart.

How My Humiliating Assessment at the Waste of Money Gym Went

1. My diet will kill me within the week according to Mr Motivator.

2. I basically need to lie face down in an allotment and graze.

3. My lung capacity is below average despite me doing £100 of not smoking.

4. Which means my dreams of being a world-class athlete are over.

5. My breaststroke kick is slightly asymmetrical. Like a lame frog.

6. In my front crawl too much energy is spent splashing apparently.

7. It's the splashing that shows how fast I'm going. Cretin!

8. My butterfly is still in the caterpillar stage. Oh ha ha ha.

9. I have above average stamina. Well above average, thank you.

10. They don't call me Mister Ultra-go-all-night-lover-man for nothing.*

    * To be honest, no one's actually called me that. But give it time.

Frank and Brutal Assessment of My Love Life

1. I fall in love too easily. It takes about four minutes on average.

2. Which is twice as long as my lovemaking. Only kidding.

3. I have mastered a range of powerful and exotic sexual techniques.

4. I just need a chance to try them out with someone properly.

5. Have slept with twelve women. Not all at once.

6. Can't really do sex without love. Or at least deep-seated affection.

7. That's one of my exotic positions – deep-seated affection.

8. Want a happy marriage like my parents but without the pointless rows.

9. Let's face it, no one will ever compare to Sabah. Ever.

10. Which means other women don't really get out of the starting gate.

What I Say When People Ask Me How I Met Abi

1. We knew each other at work. She was between my desk and the copier.

2. I copied a lot of stuff that didn't need copying.

3. I worked in exotic far-flung sites. A bit like an electrical Indiana Jones.

4. I brought her witty souvenirs back from my trips. She loved that.

5. She was impressed that I ran the Bracknell 10k in 38:50.

6. She was going out with an absolute loser called Richard.

7. Who was some kind of good-looking rugby-playing rich City type.

8. But a nob.

9. We danced together at the office Christmas party (Abi not Richard).

10. Unlike most Englishmen, I involve my hips in dancing. She was toast.

What Abi Says When People Ask Her How She Met Me

1. I couldn't work the photocopier. She sorted me.*

2. I was impressed that *she* was running the Bracknell 10k.

3. For some reason I brought her insulting gifts back from my travels.

4. When she'd clearly specified duty-free vodka.

5. My face was 'curiously endearing' (I'll take that).

6. I had the same very basic sense of humour as her dad.

7. She was at a low ebb.

8. At the office party I found the Scottish dancing incredibly confusing.

9. Her heart was moved out of sheer pity. And one too many vodkas.

10. Richard made her cry. I made her laugh. But it was a close-run thing.

   * Her first and most repeated joke. And obviously not true or funny.

Lovely Romantic Things I Did During our Whirlwind* Courtship

1. Put my last Rolo in an envelope and sent it to her recorded delivery.

2. Bought some incredibly dull postcards of Birmingham (her home town).

3. Posted them to her from Saudi Arabia, Oman, Kuwait and Kazakhstan.

4. Sent her a pizza at work with 'I Love You' picked out in pepperoni.

5. Created a 1,000-Malteser trail from her front door to her bed.

6. Where I placed beautiful new brushed-cotton PJs on her pillow.**

7. Took a three-week job in Venezuela. Sent her tickets to join me.

8. Painted a picture of some shoes she said she'd always wanted.

9. And then bought them for her on her birthday.***

10. Took her on the Orient Express to Venice. Best two days of my life.

   * More of a gentle breeze if we're honest.

   ** For use when I wasn't there.

   *** They had to go back for some technical reason.

Ten Things I'll Always Remember About the New York Marathon

1. The fleet of yellow school buses taking us to the start on Staten Island.

2. Huge barrels of free donuts at the start. And people eating them!

3. Huge barrels of Vaseline. Applying lots of that to everything that moves.

4. Having a pee with a thousand other blokes in the world's longest urinal.

5. Starting across the Verrazano Bridge with a view of the Twin Towers.

6. Running across the Brooklyn Bridge into Manhattan. Feeling pretty good.

7. Hitting the Bronx and hitting the wall at around the same time.

8. Saved by a little girl in the crowd who gave me a packet of sweets.*

9. Turning into Fifth Avenue and seeing the Empire State five miles away.

10. Finishing in Central Park in a disappointing 3:51. Eating very large pizza.

   * It's not often little girls give sweets to strangers.

Cool Dispassionate Analysis of Whether I Should Marry Abi

1. She is a good socio-economic cultural-heritage match for me.

2. She seems relatively healthy and is in good working order.

3. She has childbearing hips, as my grandmother would say.

4. Nan had seven children so she knows what she's talking about.

5. Abi's mother is a bit scary but not all women turn out like their mother.

6. Despite everything I do and say, Abi seems quite keen on me.

7. To be honest, she's actually a bit of a catch.

8. Almost out of my league if it wasn't for my lethal charm.

9. It's time I settled down. Although I don't actually feel unsettled now.

10. I love her. Which I think is probably quite important.

How I Meant to Propose to Abi

1. Amongst other things Abi has a very beautiful neck. Much like a swan.

2. Swans also mate for life. My pet name for her is Little Swan.*

3. She makes an odd noise and stretches her neck when she needs a drink.

4. I secretly found a chocolate sculptor who taught at a catering college.

5. I asked him to carve a beautiful swan from 20lb of chocolate.

6. The swan would be sitting next to a white chocolate egg.

7. In which there would be a silver ring saying 'Be my swan forever'.

8. The finished carving was totally rubbish. It looked like an angry dodo.

9. Later we went to a friend's wedding and Abi said we should get married.

10. The dodo sat in the garage for a while. Then I took it to the tip.

* Puke if you must.

Why My Running Spreadsheet is a Thing of Sublime Beauty

1. I've recorded every run for 18 years. It's the stats that keep me going.

2. I can remember up to six split times in my head while running a 10k.

3. When I'm home I input my splits and times into my master spreadsheet.

4. Which I religiously back up every Sunday after my long run.

5. I can spend hours in the bath drooling over stats. Even if they're rubbish.

6. Really I should do lots of different runs and explore the area.

7. But then I wouldn't be able to compare times so I don't.

8. Sometimes I do an incredibly fast run which smashes all my past times.

9. There's no reason for it, I just have wings for that day.

10. Life doesn't have many days like that. You have to cherish them.

Why I Warm to My Father-in-Law

1. When I asked for his daughter's hand he said, 'Take the rest of her too.'

2. My visits seem like the welcome arrival of reinforcements at a long siege.

3. He used to be an AA man (cars not alcohol). I think.

4. He is at one with the internal combustion engine.

5. He has more spanners than I have cutlery.

6. His shed smells like every shed should smell like. Sheddy.

7. He used to be a useful bantamweight boxer.

8. That doesn't mean he fought chickens. I foolishly said that.

9. His favourite question is 'Is there anything you need fixing?'

10. He calls me 'friend'. I'm not sure he remembers my name.

Why I Seem to Have a Mother-in-Law from Central Casting

1. Her factory setting is 'Look at me, I'm very upset'.

2. The smaller the thing, the more it upsets her.

3. Really gigantic insults go unnoticed. Except by Abi on her behalf.

4. Everything we've ever done is not as good as she has already done.

5. For example our engagement ring. 'Not as good as mine.'

6. Our choice of honeymoon. 'Do people still go there?'

7. I have to sleep on the new sofa in the spare room until we're married.

8. She won't take the cellophane off the new sofa 'because it's for best'.

9. We have to marry in her church otherwise she (and God) won't come.

10. Every time I speak she changes the subject. Every time. It's brutal.

My First Argument With Abi About Values

1. Abi works in HR or Human Remains as my boss Ron calls it.

2. Her speciality is Internal Communications.

3. Or listening to your stomach rumble as my boss Ron says.

4. Her biggest challenge is managing people like my boss Ron.

5. At the moment she is busy launching our new Corporate Values.

6. Which are TEAMWORK, QUALITY, PASSION, CUSTOMER, GROWTH.

7. My office mug has the old Values on. INTEGRITY has been dropped.

8. I said this was silly. She said people can only remember five.

9. I said her job was 'invisible engineering'* (and by implication useless).

10. She said I had no people skills and should work underground like my dad.

* Phrase borrowed from my friend Tom about studying philosophy.

How I Came Close to Spoiling My Ballot Paper in the Election

1. My father has always voted Conservative as 'his moral duty'.

2. He believes socialism enslaves and impoverishes those it claims to help.

3. This is when my mother usually attacks him physically.

4. She is a proud socialist and thinks Tories are basically evil.

5. Politics was not a source of sweetness and light when I was growing up

6. The twins are Lib Dems. It's how they inoculated themselves politically

7. I realised early on that it was safer to keep quiet about politics.

8. When asked I normally say I support the Spoilt Paper Party.

9. This time Alex Cartwright was on the ballot paper to be our local MP.

10. How can you not vote for someone you were at primary school with?*

    * Easily.

Interesting Things About Marriage Guidance

1. The church marrying us was keen we went to Marriage Preparation.

2. The course was run by a priest (!) and some 'happily married' people.

3. Six couples attended looking a lot happier than the 'happily married'.

4. We were divided into men and women and sent to separate rooms.

5. Obviously that was the secret of a happy marriage!!! But it wasn't.

6. We had to write a list* of possible 'pinch points' in a marriage.

7. We men covered three flipchart sheets full of likely 'pinch points'.

8. The women had seven sheets.

9. They were never referred to again. They just hung there poisonously.

10. That was it. I've had more inspiring Health and Safety briefings at work.

    * Bit of a new experience for me.

How My Marriage Was Nearly Sabotaged by Abi's Best Woman

1. Abi's hen night was organised by her best friend Penny.

2. Penny is a large mobile emotional crisis dressed in a tent.

3. I've never really liked her. And now I definitely don't.

4. Abi came back from her hen night in tears.

5. The crying continued even after the hangover had worn off.

6. She said that they'd gone to some place to have their colours done.*

7. Abi was 'winter' and would have to replace her entire wardrobe.

8. A week later I heard that the girls had 'bumped into' Richard, Abi's ex.

9. I'm pretty sure Penny orchestrated this to give them one more chance.

10. Penny feeds off these crises like a giant white maggot. So I didn't react.

    * Some shamanic thing that women do together.

Ten Highlights of My Wedding

1. My best man Tom giving me advice on marriage in Czech proverbs.

2. Seeing Abi coming up the aisle. She and her dress were breathtaking.

3. Sounds a bit wet I know but I've seen some shockers in my time.

4. Saying our vows which Abi had slightly rewritten at the last moment.

5. Seeing a room full of everyone important in my life at the same time.

6. I wrote a limerick for every single guest – 122 of them. All good.

7. Seeing Torc country dancing with my six-year-old cousin Lisa.

8. Penny's Best Woman speech which was absolutely rubbish.

9. Discovering Tom had written 'Just Married' on my sister Lucy's car.

10. Seeing my dad in tears as we left for the honeymoon.

Wonderful Memories of Our Incredible Honeymoon

1. Very long flight to Maldives in state of exhaustion.

2. Very proud of ring wearing. Felt oddly different. Very grown up.

3. Detailed post-match analysis of wedding and speeches.

4. Mine a triumph apart from one seriously misjudged but very funny line.*

5. Beautiful villa on golden palm-kissed beach. Sun, sea, sand and sex.

6. Sex and sand really don't mix. Sand follows you around everywhere.

7. Slight crisis on Day 2. I don't seem to be able to wear flip-flops.

8. My toes automatically curl up in some kind of lifting-sucking movement.

9. I have to raise my feet up as if I'm walking in treacle.

10. Abi found this absolutely hilarious. Insisted I flip-flop everywhere.

* 'I've been welcomed into Abi's family. I already feel more dysfunctional.'

How I Squeezed a Mild Existential Crisis into One Working Week

1. I turned 33 and was preparing to help Abi move into our new house.

2. It is very nice and suburban and has three bedrooms.

3. Which suddenly makes me feel enormously fertile.

4. I was supposed to have this week off but my boss Ron took it instead.

5. Probably a simple misunderstanding but it meant I had to go in to work.

6. He'd left my appraisal on my desk. The one we're supposed to discuss.

7. In the meantime Abi had to take charge of the house move.

8. One of the removal lorries must have got lost on the way.

9. Nothing I recognise as mine seems to have made it into the new house.

10. Which feels like another appraisal done in my absence.

Why I Am Absolutely Rubbish at Confrontation

1. I just want everyone to be happy. Is that too much to ask?

2. I can't take my own opinions seriously enough to get involved.

3. I'm never completely sure that I'm not actually the one in the wrong.

4. The world is full of problems. So what if my chicken goujons are cold?

5. People are normally long gone before I realise they are downright evil.

6. A big argument always feels like a rip in the fabric of the universe.

7. It takes me about three weeks to recover from any kind of spat.

8. If I start shouting I normally end in tears. Manly tears obviously.

9. I don't do small anger. It's either mild sarcasm or thermonuclear wrath.

10. I worry that me saying anything will lead straight to a knife fight.*

   * I'm pretty sure my mother-in-law carries a blade.

Ten Stupidest Things I Have Done in My Life So Far

1. Asked butcher if they use all four legs of a sheep.

2. They do but they call the front two legs shoulders.

3. The butcher looked at me as if I had a leg growing out my forehead.

4. Tried to find out what steam smells like. It smells really painful.

5. Shaved a Celtic cross into my chest hair.

6. I blame Abi for leaving her razor next to the bath.

7. Threw the grassbox of my mower away. I JUST DON'T KNOW WHY!

8. Injured myself attempting sex in shower and missed London Marathon.

9. Sending all those postcards of Birmingham to Abi. Actually pretty silly.

10. Put my pension in Equitable Life. They spent it for me. Bastards.

What We Did With a Lovely But Rather Tricky Wedding Present

1. My cousin Bella and her tattooist husband Torc came to our wedding.

2. Their wedding present was a free tattoo on the body part of our choice.

3. We agonised over what to do with this for about three months.

4. Abi refers to them as 'tramp stamps' so wasn't in a hurry to get one.

5. I thought briefly about a large 'SOUL INSIDE' on my chest.

6. Then we remembered Charlotte once told Torc she'd always wanted one.

7. Torc has a soft spot for the twins and was happy to transfer the gift.

8. He did some Korean characters on the inside of Charlotte's ankle.

9. It meant 'No'. There was no funny mistake, that's what she wanted.

10. She told Torc that it helped her to stop saying 'Yes'.*

* We spent the next three months speculating about 'yes' to what.

How Steve Baker Shocked Me More Than He Ever Did in the Past

1. I bumped into my old best friend Steve at the coach station.

2. He recognised me straight away but I didn't recognise him.

3. He looked surprisingly normal but somehow he had shrunk.

4. He told me that the Dealers had taken him into the drug scene.

5. I told him he should have called his band the Accountancy Exams.

6. He said he'd pretty much hit rock bottom and lost everything.

7. Then in a rather confusing development he'd entered local government.

8. Working in Highways with responsibility for maintaining roundabouts.

9. I said exactly what you'd expect me to say about swings etc.

10. He shrank a little bit more and I wish I'd kept my mouth shut.

A Little Insight into My Place in Abi's Universe

1. A surprisingly large subsection of women value scatter cushions.

2. To Abi a reasonable ratio of cushions to people in a room is 6:1.

3. I now know that the last thing these cushions are is scattered.

4. They are positioned carefully to 'pull a room together'.

5. Recently I attempted to make love to Abi on our cushion-rich sofa.

6. I knew something wasn't quite right during the lovemaking.

7. In my passion almost all of the cushions were in fact scattered.

8. I may even have thrown one or two around the place with gay abandon.

9. Afterwards the cushions were back in place quicker than I was.

10. Our sofa won't be vying with a Tracey Emin installation any time soon.

My Boss Ron's Finest and Darkest Hour

1. Ron led an extremely complex project rewiring an airport terminal.

2. The budget for this project was somewhere in the region of £10m.

3. Ron overcame an incredible series of complex technical obstacles.

4. There was talk of him winning some kind of IEE* award.

5. Except that he made a financial loss on the project.

6. To be honest, it was more of a smoking black hole.

7. At the board-level inquisition and inquiry Ron's legendary defence was:

8. 'Let's not pull a butterfly apart to see why it's beautiful.'

9. Ron should have known his days were numbered.

10. But numbers clearly aren't his strong suit.

   * Institute of Electrical Engineers.

Observations on Pregnancy to be Published Only After My Death

1. Pregnant women don't really expect much of men. We become useless.*

2. Small gestures can reap big rewards. Take for example morning sickness:

3. I bought Abi a pack of crackers. She was so moved she cried.

4. But is craving for pancakes legitimate? With lemon and sugar? Really?

5. First-time mums get very, very anxious about everything.

6. 'Is it OK to paint my nails or will the fumes harm the baby?'

7. Second/third-time mums seem to live on Pinot Grigio and sushi.

8. The bump is not yours. It's not hers. It's EVERYONE'S.

9. I'm getting used to complete strangers rubbing my wife intimately.

10. Maternity clothes test your ability to compliment to the very limit.

* Some of us have been training for this moment for years.

Abi's Actual Birth Plan

1. A water birth. Especially as our baby is likely to be an Aquarius.

2. Scented candles, preferably orange and cinnamon.

3. Lavender essential oils for massage and bathing.

4. Classical music playing throughout. Bach's Violin Concertos.*

5. Husband to be present throughout.

6. No painkillers, especially no epidural.

7. Husband to cut umbilical cord.

8. I would like to be standing, kneeling, on all fours or squatting.

9. I would like to avoid induction if possible.

10. I would like skin-to-skin contact straight after birth.**

   * She ignored my suggestion of 'Can You Feel It' by the Jacksons.
   ** With baby I'm assuming.

My Actual Birth Plan

1. Clean the car.

2. Park the car facing towards town.

3. Put protective blanket on passenger seat.

4. Make sure the tank is full of petrol.

5. Have plenty of change for hospital parking.

6. Map out fastest route to hospital.

7. Identify pedestrianised zones we can drive through.

8. Work out where I can go 160mph.

9. Rehearse 'I'm sorry, officer, but she's in labour'.

10. Investigate starter model railway kits.

What I Know About Fatherhood After 18 Days

1. Hospitals don't want babies back. You get to keep them!

2. Babies sleep all the time you are awake and vice versa.

3. A baby crying is as easy to ignore as Concorde in your living room.

4. Baby's poo is orange. And other weird psychedelic shades. Yuk!

5. When pooing, a baby's face goes red. I've checked if mine still does.

6. What happened before nappies? Doesn't bear thinking about.

7. When Leo cries I check food, tiredness, wind, nappy.

8. Apart from the nappy, Abi says that's what she checks with me.

9. Babies don't have breaks. 17 years 347 days until he leaves home.

10. My deepest darkest fear is that our baby looks a little bit like Hitler.

My Low Expectations of Auntie Lucy and Charlotte Are Met in Full

1. After Leo was born we got a nice card from the twins.

2. And a little cuddly toy rabbit which we called Snoozly Bunny.

3. Leo calls it Hooee and is absolutely inseparable from it.

4. We told the twins they were welcome to come and view Leo.

5. But they never have.

6. I know he's not the first baby ever born but he's quite important to us.

7. Yesterday was Leo and Hooee's first birthday.

8. Which went really well, for us at least. Party rings are delicious.

9. I'm not sure Leo realised what was going on but he seemed to have fun.

10. There was nothing from his aunts. I suspect that's how it's going to be.

How a Tiny Boy Has Flipped My World on Its Back

1. Time I have completely to myself now comes in five-minute chunks.

2. I have said goodbye to decorum forever. I'm the minder to a monkey.

3. For a monkey he needs a shocking amount of equipment.

4. I spend 13% of every day searching the house/car/garden for Hooee.

5. I am thinking 30 years ahead for my kids, 10 minutes for me.

6. Days out are planned and executed like the invasion of Normandy.

7. I am far more emotional. I was in tears writing point 5.

8. Spontaneous affection from Leo cancels all debts.

9. I have shifted up a generation and inadvertently matured.

10. Physically and mentally me and Abi are incapable of ever having sex again.

What We're Going to Call Baby Number Two

1. If it's a girl I'd like to call her Belinda. Not after the pop singer.

2. Abi went to school with a Belinda who was a bitch. So that's out.

3. Abi has had a very strong dream that she's having a boy.

4. Her friend Penny who knows everything says the bump is boy-shaped.

5. We now both agree that we're going to call him Edward. Or Eddy.

6. Sorry, Teddy. I thought she said Eddy.

7. If I'd known she meant Teddy I wouldn't have agreed to Edward.

8. She says she'll compromise with Edmund.

9. That's not a compromise, that's a completely different name.

10. And a rubbish one. Unless you're an Edmund type. Which ours won't be.

Interesting Things About Our Lovely Little Girl Amelia

1. She's a girl.

2. Very beautiful.

3. Surprisingly sweet-tempered.

4. But she doesn't sleep. Ever.

5. She's just not interested in sleep.

6. She is a night animal. She goes to sleep at 4am.

7. I am so tired I'm not going to make it to

8. Point

9. Ten.

10. Sorry.

Why We Are Moving to a Village in the Country

1. It's not really a village and it's not really the country.

2. But it's not the centre of town. You can't get a pizza delivered.

3. We want to bring up our kids so they appreciate cows, tractors, etc.

4. We will be closer to Abi's parents who will babysit under extreme duress.

5. Our money gets a larger house and a garden for theoretical vegetables.

6. There are good local schools. Correction. There is one local school.

7. It's been rated Outstanding by DEFRA. Surely that should be OFSTED.

8. We've left a lot of our friends behind. I can't remember which ones.

9. The ones worth keeping will make the pilgrimage to the country.

10. And they can meet our new rural friends. Who are all from the city.

My Top 10 Silences

1. Moments of such transcendent natural beauty that everyone shuts up.

2. Exiting into the cool night air from a party full of loud people and music.

3. Sunday afternoon when your neighbour finishes mowing his bloody lawn.

4. When, after hours of screaming, an overtired baby finally falls asleep.

5. After replacing bad shaft couplings to driven devices such as turbofans.

6. Watching a Party Political Broadcast on mute.

7. After a chess move when your opponent slowly realises he's buggered.

8. Running so smoothly that you're alone with the beating of your heart.

9. Diving into a swimming pool and gliding underwater with trunks intact.

10. With someone you're about to kiss when there is nothing left to say.

Looking Back, Where I Think My Career Went a Little Bit Wrong

1. Henry VIII* took me aside and said that I had real potential.

2. That normally meant extra menial work so I said nothing.

3. He then said that if I wanted to I could make it to senior management.

4. But I needed to reduce the fieldwork and be more office-based.

5. At the same time he said Ron was being moved to Special Projects.

6. Which is where you're basically fired but work on rewiring toasters.

7. Ron said he was now just working on the really interesting stuff.

8. Projects that other people struggled with. Did I want to help?

9. I liked Ron so I said yes. He was properly fired shortly afterwards.

10. Which left me doing small field projects that no one else wanted.

* Ron's Tudor-style boss.

How My Parents Are Shaping Up as Grandparents

1. My father insists the grandchildren should call him Grumps.

2. I've told him he's going to be called Grandpa. And now he's grumpy.

3. It turns out that my father has never changed a nappy.

4. He was visibly shocked at the contents.

5. Maybe he thought nappies were fashion items.

6. My mother sings the kids songs while playing the piano.

7. They are mostly terrified. As I was 30 years ago.

8. She does cook cakes at the drop of a scone which everyone loves.

9. To their credit they are always available for babysitting.

10. But they like to be home in bed by 10. Which is earlier than the babies.

An Insight into My Sister from a Boyfriend Who Made It Out

1. I thought Charlotte was going out with a man named Gary.

2. I don't remember much about him apart from what he does for a living.

3. When I first asked him he said 'abrasives'. He sold sandpaper.

4. I've never been able to sand anything down since without thinking of him.

5. As I very rarely sand anything down, I very rarely think about him.

6. Until I met him in Boots with a different woman who had rough heels.*

7. Gary said that he had split up with Charlotte a good two years ago.

8. He wanted marriage, kids, holidays, sex, life – that kind of thing.

9. As he spoke, Rough Heels continually shook her head and mouthed 'bitch'.

10. Which seemed harsh. Charlotte's supposed to be the nice one.

* She was buying some cream for them. I wanted to suggest sandpaper.

Secret Little Rituals I Have to Make Life More Bearable

1. I wedge myself in the corner until the shower runs hot so I avoid cold water.

2. I am physically afraid of cold water. It's like my nemesis.

3. I have three ginger nuts with my coffee. Two isn't enough. Four is too many.

4. That's absolutely allowed because ginger is virtually a medicine.

5. In the winter I put my pants on the radiator. Clean ones obviously.

6. Starting the day with warm privates makes everything seem better.

7. When I'm out and about I always park facing the direction of departure.

8. However bad the party/meeting is you're already on your way home.

9. I have been known to wear two dressing gowns at once.

10. Abi finds this odd. Three would be odd but two is actually quite sensible.

Why the Bedroom I Grew Up in Is No More

1. My room now has shelves on all sides with classics of world literature.

2. My dad took early retirement at 58 because it was too good to refuse.

3. Mum now spends a lot more time at work ('to help with the bills').

4. At first there was an absolute deluge of vegetables from the garden.

5. Dad then decided to see what the fuss was about literature.

6. He created a spreadsheet of 500 books worth reading.

7. He buys them second-hand online and then reads them, frowning.

8. Marks are awarded for story, atmosphere, characters.

9. *Middlemarch** nearly killed him. 4/10.

10. So far *Pompeii* by Robert Harris is the world's best literature. 9¾/10.

* Mum's all-time favourite book.

My 10-Point Plan for Safety at Work

1. Conduct a visual investigation before connecting meters to branch circuit.

2. Take voltage measurements using a true-rms instrument device.

3. Test for correct wiring polarity using a ground-impedance tester.

4. Test for improper neutral-ground bonds.

5. Measure the impedance of the equipment-grounding conductor.

6. Measure neutral impedance (should not exceed 0.25 ohm).

7. Measure electrical noise using an oscilloscope with a line viewer.

8. Measure electrostatic discharge with electrostatic-discharge voltmeter.

9. Capture voltage disturbances by connecting a power-line monitor.

10. Perform a harmonic analysis of voltage waveform.

My 10-Point Plan for Safety at Home

1. On returning home, check Abi for new hair, clothes, work problems.

2. Do not attempt to have an opinion until everyone has eaten.

3. Check for toys on carpet, especially wheeled ones.

4. Never attempt to change nappies standing up (man or baby).

5. Start bedtime (for kids) while you still have energy.

6. Do not attempt to skip middle part of bedtime story.

7. Never mention Abi's mother except in glowing terms.

8. Try really hard not to make glowing terms sound like heavy sarcasm.

9. Ignore anything Abi says after third vodka.

10. Before adult bedtime perform a harmonic analysis of voltage waveform.

Really Upsetting Things You See on the News

1. Famine. How can you watch that while you're eating your tea?

2. War. There is an endless supply of excuses for people to kill each other.

3. Murder. Must be quite easy to kill someone. We're quite fragile.

4. Flooding. I don't like my socks being wet let alone my house.

5. Sexual abuse. Sometimes I think penises should be licensed.

6. Corruption. What can one man do with 60 million dollars anyway?

7. Ivory hunting. Like taking your wisdom teeth out and leaving you to die.

8. Alexander Cartwright. No longer Alex. Youngest ever Defence Secretary.

9. I don't remember him playing war games when we were at primary school.

10. But then apparently he wasn't there. Perhaps he was a stealth fighter.

Why I'm Beginning to Think Tom Stole My Hollywood Career

1. Tom emailed me to say he'd got a decent part in a Hollywood film.

2. I told him that: A. He was a wanker. B. I hated him.

3. He said that was a shame because I could have shared his Winnebago.

4. I told him that by rights that Winnebago should have my name on it.

5. Because when I couldn't lead the army across the stage he got my part.

6. Just because he was good-looking and had extraordinary stage presence.

7. And I had hamstrings like steel cables and walked like a flamingo.

8. Then he got other parts, with speaking, and acting, and great reviews.

9. Which I would have got had I been able to walk for my walk-on part.

10. Obviously engineering is better but please say hello to Emily Blunt for me.

Responsible Long-Term Financial Planning Like My Dad Does

1. Because I am mature and responsible I have been checking our finances.

2. Abi is back at work three days a week which helps.

3. The cost of the nursery is equivalent to her working two days a week.

4. I have taken a lower-paid, lower-skilled job which keeps me in the UK.

5. So I can do my fair share of the childcare. I love the little stinkers.

6. We can afford a holiday in a cottage in Wales for a week off-season.

7. The mortgage is OK if we wear the same clothes for the rest of our lives.

8. We are rapidly developing an ideological commitment to state education.

9. I told Abi that things are going to work out if we're careful.

10. She told me she's pregnant. That's Wales out.

Why I Am Thinking of Changing Our New Baby's Name to 'Peace'

1. Daniel was born in a little cottage hospital with just two beds.

2. It was like a spa weekend with an incredibly painful treatment.

3. There was even a big TV in the room to watch the snooker.*

4. Daniel came out relatively easily. I stress RELATIVELY.

5. He latched on no trouble and then something miraculous happened.

6. He slept.

7. And slept and slept. When he woke up he smiled. Then slept.

8. We took him home and he slept through the night.

9. We had no idea babies could do that.

10. We might have been worried if we hadn't been utterly asleep ourselves.

* If one wasn't completely committed to the birthing process which I was.

My First Encounter with a Kebab

1. My life has been reduced to changing nappies and checking substations.

2. I do nappies during the night, substations during the day.

3. Substations are easier. They don't wriggle, cry or smell.

4. After three nappies, four hours' sleep and two substations I pull over.

5. I sleep in lay-bys with Aretha Franklin. It's the closest I get to sex.

6. I thought I was in Spanish Harlem* until someone tapped on my window.

7. It was the owner of Best Istanbul Kebabs. I was parked where he parks.

8. I moved down the lay-by to get some more sleep. He gave me a kebab.

9. I've never eaten a kebab before. Just haven't got round to it. Very nice.

10. That's the most exciting thing to report in my life at the moment.

* Greatest song by the Queen of Soul.

My Fear That My Parents Are Actually Turning into Each Other

1. My mother is now the manager of two hospices.

2. She basically raised the money for the second one.

3. It was a team effort. Which is what you say when you're in charge.

4. She is the breadwinner of the house now.

5. Even though she earns only slightly more than Dad's pension.

6. Which annoys her. She is thinking of applying for other jobs.

7. Because she has transferable skills.

8. Dad says they didn't mention transferable skills in *Middlemarch*.

9. He says she will end up working in civil engineering, possibly underground.

10. But I know she won't. Especially if Dad says she will.

A List of My Top 10 Blessings Now That I Am 42

1. We have a lovely six-year-old boy called Leo.

2. We have a beautiful four-year-old girl called Amelia.

3. We have a cheeky one-year-old boy called Daniel.

4. I am relatively healthy apart from a dodgy cruciate ligament.

5. And some kind of weird internal breakage in my ribcage.

6. Which I don't remember getting and is probably nothing but can hurt.

7. I've got a very solid if quite dull job which pays the bills.

8. I have some good friends. Including Tom who is moderately famous.

9. We own roughly 63% of a quite nice family house. With guttering issues.

10. My parents are still around, relatively healthy and helpful.

Ten Things I've Noticed About Abi's New Job

1. She works for a very large charity that does wonderful things.

2. It should be full of wonderful charitable people but it isn't.

3. The level of unpleasantness is off the scale compared to engineers.

4. Despite this she seems to be very happy.

5. I've noticed her blooming in the way pregnant women are supposed to.

6. I don't think she enjoyed the slave labour of having three kids under five.

7. She's now paid to make rational decisions in an air-conditioned office.

8. With regular breaks for coffee and lunch and a glass of wine after work.

9. She could work from home more but she generally chooses not to.

10. In some small way I feel left behind.

How a Telegram from the Queen May Have Killed My Nan

1. For the last six years Nan has been in a home.

2. She has one incredibly hot room with the television permanently on.

3. There is a crane to help lift her in and out of bed.

4. She has pictures of flowers and grandchildren all around her.

5. When she got to 100 she received a letter from Her Majesty the Queen.

6. Nan seemed to regard this as Permission to Stop.

7. She didn't get out of bed any more.

8. More seriously she didn't bother looking at the *Radio Times*.

9. I was there when she died. Each breath became more sporadic.

10. And then there wasn't another one. I felt her spirit leave the room.*

   * Not in the engineering textbooks, but that's what I felt.

Realistically What the Best Things About Kids Are

1. They love you unconditionally because you're their dad.

2. Even when you deliberately kill off Thomas the Tank Engine.

3. Because you're so sick of him and his mates that your eyeballs bleed.

4. They carry your vital genetic inheritance (splayed toes) on to eternity.

5. They say things that are fantastically rude with no malice whatsoever.

6. You can tickle children and they laugh. Unlike your boss.

7. They remind you quite often that you are neither funny nor clever.

8. Or interesting, or cool, or hip, or technologically literate.

9. They get excited about life. And that is contagious. Up to about 8pm.

10. They're going to be paying for your nursing home.

Drawbacks of Children Prospective Parents Should Be Aware Of

1. Your beautifully arranged life is completely and utterly destroyed.

2. Children pull stickiness from the air and smear it on EVERYTHING.

3. They make noise four times greater than their bodyweight. Continuously.

4. They will never return a toy to its place until they too are parents.

5. Thomas the Tank Engine is torture. He is SO ACHINGLY DULL.

6. Kids are very expensive, especially if you choose to feed and clothe them.

7. They bicker incessantly without ever coming to a reasonable compromise.

8. The only silence you'll ever get is when you ask who broke something.

9. Kids have an extraordinary capacity to highlight adult hypocrisy.

10. Even when you've explained that it's one rule for you, another for them.

Things It's Impossible to Explain to People Who Don't Have Kids

1. It's not important what I do for a living.

2. It's not important what I eat.

3. It's not important what I wear.

4. It's not important what I say or think or feel.

5. I have to get that food into that mouth.

6. I have to change the nappy otherwise that smell will kill someone.

7. I have to fold a double buggy into a small car with one hand.

8. I have to strap three kids into seats without banging my head.

9. I have to have moist wipes within arm's reach 24 hours a day.

10. I have to read and reread *THOMAS THE SODDING TANK ENGINE*.

Phrases I've Suddenly Noticed Comprise 90% of My Conversation

1. How's it going?

2. It's all go.

3. There you go.

4. Fair enough.

5. Gosh.

6. You're joking.

7. Indeed.

8. Tell me about it.

9. That's just the way it is.

10. Mustn't keep you.

Why I Still Write Lists

1. If I didn't I would be standing in a cupboard shouting.

2. I write what I feel first. I immediately feel better.

3. Then I write what I think. Chew things over a bit.

4. Then I coolly analyse my feelings. Might blow my nose at this point.

5. I then consider what I should do about the situation.

6. I might then make some impressive promises to myself.

7. Then I tell myself to get real. It's me we're talking about.

8. At point 8 I normally run out of points.

9. But this is when the calm extra thought arrives.

10. And then we can move on relatively sensibly.

Why Arguments with Abi Seem to Be in Reverse

1. Out of the blue she suddenly bursts into tears and runs out of the room.

2. I go up and see her. She shouts at me and says I don't understand.

3. I try really hard to understand but then get confused and angry.

4. We talk at the same time round in circles. The same circles every time.

5. Then we hear one of the kids and we stop.

6. We do a lot of sniffing and gulping and try hard to calm down.

7. Then we manage to say what's on our mind.

8. Tissues are deployed and we clear ourselves up.

9. Excuses are offered normally featuring overtiredness.

10. Points accepted we then go back downstairs. Tea/vodka is made.

The Truth About Engineers

1. Nothing really happens anywhere without an engineer involved.

2. Even if you're on a bench kissing – bench installed by engineer.

3. Just because I'm an engineer doesn't mean I can fix your toaster.

4. If an engineer talks too much, run away. Something will fall down.

5. Some of the most creative people in the world are engineers.

6. But we hide it under our hard-hats and industrial-strength modesty.

7. Getting the right answer is critical for an engineer.

8. Engineers always want a solution. Even to complex emotional stuff.

9. Which is why engineers don't understand complex emotional stuff.

10. Something is going wrong in my marriage and I can't fix it.

What Happens When Abi Goes Up to See Her Friend Penny

1. I look after the kids. There are tears and tantrums. But they don't mind.

2. We all watch the *Battle of Britain* DVD which the kids love.

3. I wonder what part of our marriage will be put under the microscope.

4. I quietly empathise with Penny's husband Terry who is in a bad bad place.

5. Abi returns energised like she's had a big workout which she kind of has.

6. After a while Abi starts using words and phrases she's never used before.

7. The fat patronising presence of Penny will then be in the room.

8. I try to work out which relationship theory is being applied to me.

9. Abi has a large vodka. Uses more new phrases. Starts crying.

10. I go and change Dan's nappy as it seems simpler and less messy.

Why I Sometimes Get Really Really Sick of Myself

1. Everything I say is boring rubbish and often borderline offensive.

2. I'm not a good friend to my good friends.

3. I don't have a bucket list of exciting things to tick off.

4. And that's from the person with a million lists. Pathetic.

5. I don't floss. It frightens me. I do not want to saw my head off.

6. I have the willpower of a small sickly gnat.

7. That's probably offensive to gnats. They've bitten most of Scotland.

8. My body is like the bit you cut off bacon. Before you've fried it.

9. The distribution of my hair is ridiculous. What am I evolving into?

10. I am an ungrateful, whining, self-indulgent, flabby sofa monkey.

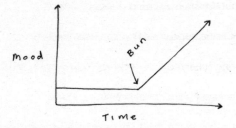

How I Feel After I've Eaten

1. Much better.

2. Things really aren't that bad.

3. It annoys me that I'm such a simple animal.

4. That my world can be hugely improved by two slices of toast.

5. And one chocolate éclair.

6. Or two éclairs because they're not actually that big.

7. And I deserve it.

8. Because I've got a lot of issues to deal with.

9. Which aren't actually that bad.

10. Now that I've eaten.

Why I Visited the SS *Great Britain* Twice in One Day

1. We visited SS *Great Britain* in Bristol, a great day out for the family.

2. Especially families who need to be shown Britain's engineering history.

3. It was a pretty successful day until we all got home.

4. And realised that Leo's rabbit Hooee had been left somewhere in Bristol.

5. I offered Leo the spare rabbit which he threw across the room in disgust.

6. The SS *Great Britain* was about to close but I just got there in time.

7. A wonderful lady called Sylvia had found Hooee and stored him safely.

8. I wanted to marry Sylvia right there and then.

9. Instead I gave her the spare rabbit which was perfect for her nephew.

10. I am sure there's some kind of karmic lesson there.*

    * No idea what it is.

Anecdotes I Must Stop Telling Because Even I Find Them Boring

1. The one about the iguana on the ceiling fan.

2. The one about me throwing away my lawnmower grassbox.

3. The one about me sharing a lift with Roger Moore.

4. The one about the randy charging cow and Abi hurdling barbed wire.

5. The one about me inadvertently mooning on White Horse Hill.

6. The one about me being at school with the Rt Hon. Alexander Cartwright.

7. The one about me crossing into China without a visa.

8. The one about me as a kid putting unwanted sprouts in the freezer.

9. The one about me running over the woman in the big yellow dress.

10. And how her going over the top of my car was like a Shell carwash.*

   * I'll probably keep telling this one.

Why I Have Taken a Job in Libya

1. I am sick of substations. And the crap people throw into them.

2. I actually miss oil rigs. They're big with interesting wiring and people.

3. This job will last three months which is a long time away from home.

4. But it will pay the equivalent of two and a half years of substations.

5. Abi's parents will come and help look after the kids.

6. Abi's dad has volunteered to come with me to Libya.

7. I will miss the kids horribly but this is for their benefit.

8. Abi said, 'It will be like a trial separation.' I think she was joking.

9. A small guilty part of me is looking forward to getting away.

10. It will be like a beach holiday without the sea. Probably.

How I Learned to Swear in Spanish

1. Libya is bigger than Europe. It also has more gas and oil than Europe.

2. I am in the far south where there is lots of nothing. Except oil.

3. I live with 500 expats in a Portakabin city with no alcohol or women.

4. If I wanted to become a monk this would be good training.

5. I am powering up new oil wells. My boss is a Mexican with issues.

6. In the morning I drive him to the rigs while he curses Libya.

7. At lunchtime I drive him back to base where he curses his ex-wife.

8. After siesta we curse humanity, especially Panamanians. No reason given.

9. Back to work cursing sand, flies, heat, gringos, Land Rovers and in-laws.

10. Drive back with undiluted continuous swearing at random targets.

My Understanding of Advanced Theoretical Physics*

1. The force of gravity attracts objects together like a falling apple.

2. That's because mass causes the space–time continuum to bend.

3. Like someone heavy lying in the middle of a soft mattress.

4. Small objects then roll towards larger objects like Maltesers in bed.

5. But if you're inside the apple things look different. It's all relative.

6. What happens in the subatomic structure of the apple is even odder.

7. Things happen and don't happen at the same time.

8. Which makes time itself look rather flexible.

9. Thankfully the speed of light is a constant. At the moment.

10. But probably wasn't before the Big Bang. So that's all clear.

* Written in the middle of a three-day Saharan shamal (sandstorm) in a competition with myself to write the most difficult list.

How Abi Coped With Me Being Away for Three Months

1. She did a brilliant job.

2. Her mum was actually very helpful.

3. She looked after the kids a lot.

4. So that Abi could have a bit of a break.

5. Mostly with her new friend Adrian from work.

6. Who was also very helpful.

7. Very.

8. Helpful.

9. Indeed.

10. The kids have shot up. I'm never leaving them that long again.

Why I'm Pulling the Plug on My Engineering Career

1. I have started giving substations pet names.

2. I have calculated enough service loads and arc-flash-incident energies.

3. I've seen all the motor-control panel boards I ever want to see.

4. I'm getting tired of wearing flame-retardant underpants.

5. I spend hours every day trying to clear my email inbox.

6. Abi has asked for a divorce. That was also in my inbox.

7. I want to see my children more than every other weekend.

8. The more you earn, the more you pay, the less you see your kids.

9. I'm not going to work to pay for the privilege of not seeing them.

10. They'll be gone before I know it. I need to be here for them now.

Interesting Things About Marriage Guidance (Part 2)

1. The Relate meetings are held in the office of a local law firm.

2. Which is like having a doctors' surgery based in a mortuary.

3. They want you to get better but it's feeding time if you don't.

4. Our counsellor asked us what we wanted to get from the session.

5. We beat around a few bushes and raked over a few coals.

6. She asked us if we wanted to stay together. There was a silence.

7. And then Abi's stomach made a sound like a washing machine draining.

8. On the way home we agreed to divorce and then popped into Tesco's.

9. We did the divorce without lawyers with a DIY pack from WHSmith.

10. It cost us £75. Plus more than half of everything I've ever earned ever.

Where I Was When the Rt Hon. Alexander Cartwright Lost His Seat

1. In my seat. The sofa in my new divorced-dad mini-house.

2. He had a lovely smile on his face when the results were being read out.

3. Until he realised he'd lost.

4. Or rather that someone else who wasn't him had won.

5. He still had the exact same smile but it wasn't lovely any more.

6. My psychologist friend says he has Narcissistic Personality Disorder.

7. He can't register any reality that's not entirely favourable to himself.

8. The voters did that job for him.

9. It was a lovely moment. But not for him.

10. But he'll be back because he's made of unsinkable material.

How the Valley of Death Isn't All Bad

1. My friend Tom's Hollywood film never got green-lighted.

2. Which meant that it was never made and nor was Tom's career.

3. While he was waiting for his next audition he went on a road trip.

4. In Death Valley he stopped to take a photo in a place called Badwater.

5. And got talking to a couple of British girls on holiday.

6. One of whom (Alice, very nice) he's now engaged to.

7. Who lives about eight miles from me.

8. Where Tom has now also moved to.

9. Doing his exciting new job in PR.

10. So much for my career as his bag carrier/Emily Blunt attendant.

Jobs I'm Considering While Sitting in Empty House* With No Kids

1. Hit man. One-off jobs on people mainly called Adrian.

2. Electrical engineer. Yes, I know I've just given that up. Shut up.

3. But I had a salary and beautiful benefits. Pension! Health care! Friends!

4. Writer. Action-packed novels based on globetrotting electrical engineer.

5. Tesco checkout. I'm a people person. Except for the one I married.

6. English teacher. I can brush up on my Marxism.

7. Electrical engineering consultant. Like my old job but with no benefits.

8. Actor. Playing Everyman electrical-engineering-type roles.

9. Dog walker. With or without dog. That's what I'm currently doing.

10. Electrical engineer.

* Scatter cushion to person ratio 0:1.

Skills Needed to Access 'Easy Open' Ready Meals for One

1. First-class engineering degree, preferably mechanical.

2. Instruction-decoding capability of Bletchley Park.

3. Three-inch sharpened nails on at least seven fingers.

4. Pulling-apart power of 24 horses in each direction.

5. Applied twisting power of nuclear submarine's main turbine shaft.

6. Microscopic vision to see PULL HERE label. Braille skills to locate end.

7. Patience of St Enduro, patron saint of the incredibly patient.

8. Basic butchery skills in handling large extremely sharp knives.

9. Karate black belt for application of immense force in single blow.

10. First-aid knowledge to treat inadvertent but serious self-harm.

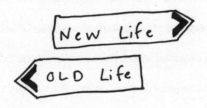

What Being Divorced Feels Like

1. An incredibly tedious ruinously expensive catastrophe.

2. An unmitigated confusing unnecessary disaster for the kids.

3. A brutal destruction of all your assumptions about the rest of your life.

4. Nights with nothing to do but view the smoking wreck of your life.

5. A surprising lack of young women making themselves instantly available.

6. A great way of getting rid of your ex-wife's interior-decor choices.*

7. A catastrophic deterioration in your diet/health/finances.

8. A mixture of incredible anger at/mild sympathy for Adrian.

9. How has he earned the right to spend time with my kids? He hasn't.

10. But when the kids are with me I've never felt closer to them.

* And mother-in-law. That's almost worth everything else put together.

How to Avoid Talking to People About Your Divorce

1. Hide if you can. Run away if you have to.

2. Pretend you haven't seen them. Look sideways for no reason.

3. If they spot you, wave, then cross the road through heavy traffic.

4. Speed up your walking. Say 'Hi' just as you pass them. Dart into shop.

5. Say 'I mustn't keep you' after four seconds of conversation.

6. Feign a migraine that makes eye contact/talking impossible.

7. Say 'Indeed' and walk off as if nothing more could possibly be said.

8. Hide in your house with all the lights off. Muffle your breathing.

9. Get your post redirected. Consider extensive plastic surgery. Emigrate.

10. Or say it was just one of those things and you wish Abi the best of luck.

How Lucy's New Boyfriend Makes My Heart Sing with Joy

1. I took my parents round to Lucy's house to meet new boyfriend Ian.

2. He seemed relatively normal for a Lucy boyfriend. If slightly nervous.

3. Everything went smoothly until he wanted to show us something online.

4. He brought his laptop over which had a 22ft lead to the broadband hub.

5. I asked him whether his laptop could do Wi-Fi. It looked quite new.

6. 'Wi-Fi makes you impotent,' he said. That's when I began to like Ian.

7. He also has his mobile in a protective pouch against radio waves.

8. Which 'affect your mental wave patterns'. I love that man.

9. Lucy's expression dared me to make fun of him. Would I do that?

10. I asked Ian how he was protecting himself from the microwave.

My First Holiday with All the Kids as a Single Dad

1. I took us all to Majorca on a Single Parent package holiday.

2. The flight was stupidly early, the transfer incredibly long.

3. When we arrived at the hotel Daniel was beside himself with tiredness.

4. Our room wasn't ready.

5. Daniel started to scream. He kept screaming for an hour.

6. In front of hundreds of holidaymakers from all over the world.

7. I finally got a few chips inside him. He perked up and then conked out.

8. I lay in bed thinking I will never survive seven days of this.

9. Especially if they get covered in sand. I considered changing our flight.

10. I felt better at breakfast. By the end of the week I was almost relaxed.

How I Am Now Virtually a Theatre Writer/Producer/Director

1. I drove at 94mph down the M40. I blame Luther Vandross.*

2. Had a choice of £100 fine or attending Speed Awareness Course.

3. I spent 18 years not smoking to earn £100. So it was The Course.

4. Met 23 other people on the course strangely united by speed.

5. One was late because 'he'd been driving so slowly'.

6. The course was rubbish. Patronising. Boring. Counterproductive.

7. I told my policeman mate on the school gates. He agreed.

8. I redesigned the course. It took me one evening while listening to music.

9. Actually 'Driver's Seat' by Sniff 'n' the Tears. Good speeding music.

10. Got the gig. That's what I now do for a living. Boof!

* 'Searching' – brilliant song when he was lead singer of Change.

What I Really Had to Do to Get the Gig

1. Meet the wrong person three times before he admitted it wasn't him.

2. Wait three months to see the right person.

3. Attend six separate meetings with groups of unimpressed civil servants.

4. Put myself through a lengthy government tendering process.

5. Designed specifically to baffle, intimidate and degrade the will to live.

6. Reformat my proposal three different times in three different ways.

7. Pass a range of background checks relating to credit, crime and sexuality.

8. Spend time with Road Traffic Officers (only bright spot).

9. Run three pilot sessions at my own expense.

10. Sign a contract so complex my lawyer was reduced to tears.

Biscuits in Order of Their Therapeutic Value

1. Jammie Dodgers. But not the satanic imitation jam rings.

2. Custard Creams. Three taken with tea. Twice if necessary.

3. Ginger Nuts. A morning biscuit with coffee at 10.30am.

4. Coconut Rings. As many as you can fit on your little finger.

5. Chocolate Hobnobs. Basically a healthy oatmeal snack

6. Fruit Shortcake. Eat by inserting whole biscuit in mouth.*

7. Chocolate Chip Cookies. Ideally freshly baked with melting chocolate.

8. Iced Party Rings. Best eaten just before serving at children's party.

9. Jaffa Cakes. Orangey spongey chocolatey cakey biscuity round thing.

10. Rich Tea. Only to be contemplated in absolute dire emergencies.

* Ron taught me this pioneering technique at work.

Options for What to Do With Your Wedding Ring After Divorce

1. Put it in the back of a drawer and forget about it.

2. Along with all the vows about being together until death did us part.

3. Take it to a place that says WE BUY GOLD. And get about £15.

4. Keep it for your children. To remind them of the divorce.

5. Melt it down and have it refashioned into a belly-button stud.

6. Take it down to the river on a glorious sunny day.

7. Walk to the centre of the old stone bridge.

8. Forgive yourself and your ex. Drop the ring into the river.

9. Avoiding ducks.

10. Watch the river continue to flow serenely on, just like life.

Contents of My 'Important Documents' File at Home

1. My will is in an envelope marked 'Last Willy and Testicle'.

2. Abi thought this was inappropriate. I call it having the last laugh.

3. My birth certificate. I was a boy. Still am.

4. Two old British passports. Big blue beauties that you could surf on.

5. Letter from my Great Uncle Percy who was killed in World War I.

6. Old Post Office savings book. £36 withdrawn to pay for first bike.

7. National insurance card with strangely memorable number.

8. Immunisation record. With boosters. Some late typhus shots.

9. Marriage certificate. Four birth certificates.* Divorce certificate.

10. Counterpart driving licence. Two speeding endorsements. Totally unfair.

* We lost one. Ben. He was with us four days then got meningitis.

Why I Can't Talk About Ben

1. Because the only other person who knew him was Abi.

2. And I no longer speak to her.

3. Because we're divorced.

4. It's a black hole we share.

5. We weren't doing particularly well.

6. But that finished us off.

7. I don't even have a photo of him.

8. I loved Ben and I still do.

9. And one day I hope I'll be with him again.

10. And that's it really.

Why It's Never a Good Idea to Look Up Your Ex-Girlfriends Online

1. Sabah doesn't exist online. She's gone. I'm kind of glad.

2. Becky Hatton is a Tory councillor. Campaigning for school buses.

3. Emma Standish is dead. I remember her blonde hair flowing as she ran.

4. I always meant to go out with her. But she was out of my league.

5. And now she's permanently out of all leagues. Deeply depressing.

6. Ruth is divorced from Lance Adams. The professional footballer.

7. Andrea sings in a choir and married a bass. She looks happy.

8. But online everyone looks happy. It's like a big glossy brochure.

9. We need a site where everyone looks tired, disappointed and crushed.

10. That would cheer everyone up.

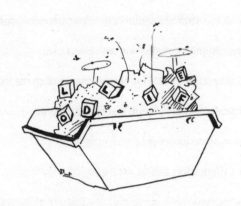

An Unexpected Archaeological Find from a Past Life

1. After the divorce we sold our family house and got a skip.

2. To throw out all the stuff we couldn't fit in our two new smaller homes.

3. I did a very thorough job of clearing my things out.

4. Probably too thorough. I put a lot of personal stuff in the skip.

5. Pictures and prints I wish I'd kept. But they all went

6. In fact anything with sentimental value went.

7. Looking back I think I was self-harming.

8. One thing that survived the purge was the fortune-teller's cassette.

9. I listened to it again and she had it spot on about tragedy and recovery.

10. But then maybe all lives are like that.

How Ian Created a Highly Charged Atmosphere

1. Lucy had been going out with Insulated Ian for about three years.

2. During that time Charlotte was seeing Derek of the hidden personality.

3. They often went out as a foursome in Ian's electric vehicle.*

4. One day Ian casually rested his hand on Charlotte's thigh.

5. Electricity flowed. No honestly it didn't. Sorry.

6. Lucy saw it. Ian said it was a case of mistaken identity.

7. Which is absolutely the worst thing he could have said.

8. Lucy binned off Ian. Who then asked Charlotte out.

9. She said yes. It lasted three weeks. Not sure what happened to Derek.

10. The twins now have an unspoken agreement not to speak to each other.

* Just kidding! Actually a Renault Laguna.

How It Feels Sleeping with Someone New After Years of Marriage

1. It's a little bit like getting in a rental car.

2. It's still a car but nothing's quite where you expect it to be.

3. You have to adjust various things to get comfortable.

4. You then discover that it does some exciting things your old car didn't.

5. And you wonder how you ever got along without those things.

6. There might be one or two things your new car doesn't do.

7. Which your old car did.

8. But you were tired of those things anyway.

9. Once you get the hang of your new car, it's good fun.

10. But then you hand it back. And your garage is still empty.

Important Things to Look for in 'New Wife' According to My Kids

1. She has to make at least three basic meals.

2. Must smell nice but not of lavender.

3. She can have strong opinions but not all of the time.

4. She has to at least do some stuff.

5. She can't be a girly girl saying 'bring me some glitter'.

6. She needs to have Aztec beliefs. Willing to make sacrifices.

7. Must be able to engage in banterous conversation.

8. Her milkshake must bring all the boys to the yard.

9. No pets that we don't know.

10. No silly permanent life-attitude stuff.*

    * Daniel – quite incisive for an eight-year-old.

How the Dating Website Interpreted This Brief for Me

1. Diana – 39 – no kids. Loves walking, country pubs, cinema.

2. Paula – 43 – 2 kids. Loves cinema, walking, country pubs.

3. Toni – 42 – 1 kid. Loves glass of wine. Quiet nights in. Walking dog.

4. Rebecca – 41 – 2 kids. Loves DVDs, minibreaks, cinema.

5. Jemima – 44 – 3 kids. Loves country walks, eating out, minibreaks.

6. Sarah – 48 – no kids at home. Loves travel, eating out, country pubs.

7. Anita – 47 – 2 kids. Loves walking the dog. Quiet nights in.

8. Niamh – 44 – 3 kids. Loves walking the dog. Country pubs.

9. Anoushka – 24 – very nice. Wants to meet gentlemens for pampering.*

10. Jane – 49 – 2 kids. Loves quiet nights in. Glass of wine. Country walks.

* Slightly different site.

How for a Brief Moment I Thought I Was a Great Lover

1. I went to a salsa class because it's a great place to learn salsa.

2. And meet women. Like Vanessa.

3. After a few warm-up moves we ended up in bed.

4. Unless she is a very convincing actress, she came almost immediately.

5. I thought she just wanted to get an early bus home, but no.

6. This happened every time. Virtually anything would set her off.

7. I just had to clear my throat and she would be writhing in ecstasy.

8. I really can't take any kind of credit. I was just an interested bystander.

9. But she did like me telling her dirty stories which also did the trick.

10. When I found myself reworking *Thomas the Tank Engine* I called it a day.

How Online Dating Is Beginning to Feel Like Electrical Engineering

1. The computer tells me what part of the network (person) I'm visiting.

2. When I reach the location I do an immediate visual inspection.

3. Then I check the wiring. Nine times out of 10 everything is normal.

4. Normal women, normally wired, working normally. So I go home.

5. What I'm looking for is random electricity. Something not earthed.

6. Just a spark or a live wire. Which is dangerous but also exciting.

7. And then it would get interesting. And I could get my toolbox out.

8. But normally it's normal. We connect and then we disconnect.

9. There is no surge. The lights don't go on suddenly. Or off.

10. Perhaps it's best when things just hum safely in the background.

How We Built this Village on Motown, Soul and Disco

1. Tom came round to chat through his divorce over a few beers.

2. I got him to help me put together a netball hoop for Amelia.

3. We had a few beers and listened to my playlist on Spotify.

4. 'Sail On' by the Commodores came on. I said it was my divorce song.

5. I sang the whole thing very loud and very hammy. It helps.

6. Then we belted it out together. To be honest, we were a bit squiffy.

7. He emailed me the day after saying we should form a Dads' Soul Choir.

8. Like the Commitments but for dads with a lot of commitments.

9. I think he was joking. But if there's one thing I take seriously it's jokes.

10. It's a pretty solid idea. Unlike the netball hoop which is a bit wonky.

My New Awesome Social Media Marketing Machine

1. I cooked pancakes for my kids. I am a god with a frying pan.

2. I mentioned the Dads' Soul Choir in a very offhand way.

3. They said it was a great idea as long as I didn't sing.

4. Or attempt to dance. And I should stand at the back.

5. I said Tom would be the front man. They thought that was brilliant.*

6. They said I should advertise it on Facebook.

7. I said I would rather feed my genitals to a leaf shredder.**

8. Later that evening Leo showed me the Dads' Soul Choir site he made.

9. The kids then spread the word on Instasnapgrambuzzvinetube.

10. By the time I went to bed 11 dads had signed up. That's a choir!

* Really beginning to dislike Tom.

** Or words to that effect.

Entry Requirements for the Dads' Soul Choir

1. You have to be a dad.*

2. You get a 10% discount for every child.**

3. You have to have Dad rhythm and Dad soul.

4. You have to have had the Dad blues.

5. You have to feel the Dad force.

6. You have to have been to Funky Town.

7. You have to have R.E.S.P.E.C.T. for Aretha Franklin.

8. You're particularly welcome if you're D.I.V.O.R.C.E.D.

9. You must dance in a way which deeply embarrasses your children.

10. Big fans of Morrissey need not apply.

   * Women welcome too (if they're a dad).
   ** Up to a maximum of 10.

Our Serious Semi-Professional Auditions for A Choir Leader

1. The first guy had a bow tie. NO! NO! NO! NO! NO! NO! NO!

2. The second guy asked us what we wanted to get out of the choir.

3. We said singing. He asked if we were trying to work out some issues.

4. The third guy asked us what we meant by soul. Did it include Debussy?

5. I told him to close the door on the way out. What a Clair de Loony!

6. Then there was a lady. She looked like Ruby Turner* but wasn't.

7. She coolly eyed us 14 men as if we were the veriest trash.**

8. She then told us to stand up. I for one wasn't arguing.

9. Half an hour later we were singing 'What a Feeling!' from *Flashdance*.

10. Our new Choir Mistress is Deborah. I am totally in love with her.

   * British soul legend.
   ** Which to be honest ...

My Growing Realisation That Some Women Are a Bit Odd in Bed

1. Rachel was someone I danced salsa with. Rather well actually.

2. There was one complex move which required us to get unethically close.

3. Soon we were recreating this move in bed in a slightly more naked way.

4. When Rachel dances salsa she always counts the beats out loud.

5. Which I discovered she also does in bed.

6. It's difficult to be natural when your partner's saying 'one and two'.

7. It's also quite exhausting after a while. Like British Military Fitness.

8. You begin to hope she'll get to 'three and four' and call it a day.

9. But she never did. It was continuous 'one and two and one and two'.

10. And when we stopped she cried. Very disconcerting and not very Latin.

What I Think About Being 50

1. Only halfway to being 100. Need to conserve energy.

2. I'm now in the youth of old age. Still doesn't sound good.

3. But I'm glad to see the back of my forties. They were hard work.

4. I haven't got another marathon in me. My brain has. My legs haven't.

5. I need the bus pass now while I can still get upstairs.

6. Death is beginning to take an interest in my generation. Bugger off.

7. My 10-year-old self is still perfectly preserved inside.

8. I seemed to have stopped worrying about everything. Quite liberating.

9. I feel I still have one huge act of jaw-dropping grandeur in me.

10. One final shot at immortality. If I can find my glasses.

How My Running Career Ended With a Bang

1. Kids away with mother so booked myself fitness holiday in St Lucia.

2. Did exercise bootcamp on beach every morning at 7am.

3. Got extra keen and signed up for yoga stretches at 6am.

4. Stretched more than I've ever stretched anything before ever.

5. Ran along beach with young beautiful people. Kept up no problem.

6. Felt the power returning and accelerated after young blonde.

7. Heard bang. Assumed I'd been shot. Fell into sea. Thought I'd drown.

8. Fished out by young fit men. One of them was an orthopaedic surgeon.

9. He looked at my leg, said 'You're buggered'. Achilles tendon snapped.

10. Wheelchair to airport. Inserted into airplane via catering trolley.

What I've Learned After Two Months on Crutches

1. I've swapped my car for an automatic so I can still drive.

2. An automatic makes you drive sedately. It's like ageing 20 years.

3. Disabled parking spots are really really important if you can't walk.

4. Stairs are everywhere. 'Up with the good. Down with the bad.'

5. On crutches that's how you remember which leg to lead with.

6. Otherwise you end up in a heap at the bottom. Or back in hospital.

7. At home I propel myself round on an office chair with wheels.

8. My kids sometimes wheel me into a dark corner. A preview of old age.

9. Going to the loo is a combination of gymnastics and drive-by shooting.

10. On the bright side my upper body has muscles I've never seen before.

Reasons Why I Am Never Rude About Trainspotters

1. I am one. Secretly. Like all men. But I'm increasingly out.

2. We'd all like our life to run on rails. With a powerful engine.

3. And exotic destinations. Like Adlestrop. And Doncaster.

4. Serial killers are never trainspotters. It's one or the other.

5. Then I watched a new programme on TV about rail journeys.

6. The sort of journeys I'd like to be taking with the family.*

7. It was presented by the ex-Rt Hon. Alexander Cartwright. Now Alex.

8. Who I didn't go to primary school with. How did he get that gig?

9. When there are a million men more trainspottier than him.

10. His smile was the same. But this time he was genuinely happy.

    * If I had an entirely different family that loved trains.

Possible Things My Mum's 'Interesting Development' Could Be

1. She's pregnant. Highly unlikely at 73. But I would welcome a sibling.

2. She's coming out. Possible. She's always been close to Hilary Barnet.

3. She and Dad are getting divorced. Finally snapped about 'concierge' gag.

4. She's won an enormous amount of money. I've already spent it mentally.

5. They are bankrupt because they have fallen victim to a scam. More likely.

6. Your sisters are not really your sisters. Quite relaxed about that one.

7. Selling up and buying a narrow boat. Unlikely. Dad needs to dig potatoes.

8. I'm actually adopted. Nope. I can see where my splayed toes come from.

9. Cancer. That's probably what it is. Really don't want that at all.

10. They've got a cat. It'll be that. Mum's been desperate for one for years.

How God Singled Out My Father for Special Treatment

1. His train was severely delayed. Got talking to a man on platform.

2. Heard about model railway exhibition in town hall that Sunday.

3. Went to town hall but entered wrong room where people were praying.

4. Too embarrassed to leave. Was called to front by 'priestess'.

5. Hands were laid on him. He focused on retaining his wallet.

6. Felt strange. Broke down in floods of tears. Group hug.

7. Blinding light and feelings of fathomless joy and wonder.

8. Dad now goes to church twice every Sunday and some weekdays.

9. Talks about Priestess Henrietta continuously. Prays before tea.

10. Mum has closed their joint current account just in case.

How I Am Very Rapidly Instilling in My Children a Love of Culture

1. I have introduced a concept called 'Speed museum/gallery/exhibition'.

2. We're only allowed 50 minutes in total not including tea room/gift shop.

3. All galleries/rooms have to be covered. Running is not allowed.

4. Each child has to stop at two exhibits and say, 'This is fascinating.'

5. They then have to say why it interests them. Irony is prohibited.

6. There must be at least 100 paces between exhibits to prevent cheating.

7. I am allowed 'to be boring' about one exhibit for 3 minutes.

8. They earn £5 to lash out in tea room/gift shop as they see fit.

9. We did the British Museum in 51 minutes. Very pleased with that.

10. It's actually quite good exercise but that's not how I sell it.

My Mugs in Descending Order of Drinking Preference

1. Plain white with fat rim. Like kissing someone with lovely lips.*

2. Large Starbucks mug for weekend milky coffee (yes I did pay for it).

3. Small/medium mug with Bournville logo. Good for small strong coffee.

4. 'Comfort Diner' mug from America. Recreates authentic diner experience.

5. St Lawrence Church fundraising mug. My grandad (RIP) designed it.

6. Blue Sainsbury's mugs. Perfect size for second meditative tea of day.

7. Union Jack mug. Has to have tea in really if we're going to be British.

8. Flowery mug with delicate handle. Secretly wants to be a refined cup.

9. 'World's Best Dad'. I'm sorry but I just don't like the design.**

10. Fat ugly hand-painted mug from craft shop with earhole for handle.

* I didn't say this list wasn't going to be sad and pathetic.
** Very tricky as this was present from Amelia.

Breakthrough Moments in the Progress of Civilisation

1. Arable farming was the first one so we didn't have to hunt and gather.

2. Metalworking for swords and ploughshares and attractive jewellery.

3. The invention of the wheel for carts, wheelbarrows, scooters.

4. Movable type and printing. For books and pamphlets and junk mail.

5. Discovery of gunpowder to allow mass killing/firework displays.

6. Scientific revolution for working out things with rulers, maths, etc.

7. The Industrial Revolution for steel, steam power, railways.

8. Medical revolution for preventing/curing unpleasant diseases.

9. Technological revolution for computers, TV, Internet, Grand Theft Auto.

10. Alan's idea that the Dads' Soul Choir should throw a few shapes.*

* Have a few dance moves.

Why Alan Is the Last Person You Would Expect Moves From

1. Alan sells the alerts for trucks that say 'Caution Vehicle Reversing'.

2. He can say it in five different languages. And he does. Often.

3. He used to sell reflective chevrons for trucks until his big break.

4. He has the thickest skin of any animal not technically armoured.

5. When he's drunk he becomes totally still apart from his drinking arm.

6. Every Sunday he jogs five miles slower than he can walk it.

7. His wife 'works nights' although no one has ever seen her.

8. One night he showed us a move he'd been working on.

9. We knew he couldn't be drunk because he did actually move.

10. Deborah got us all doing it to 'Going Back to My Roots'.*

   * Odyssey obviously. The intro would make a dead man dance.

How Crime and Punishment Works in the Digital Age

1. Daniel (10) really wanted me to buy him some superhero DVD.

2. I said that was out of the question because it had a 15 certificate.

3. He did some very high-pressure wide-eyed wheedling.

4. I decided to stick to my guns. Yes, I know it was only a 15 not an 18.

5. But still. Sometimes you've got to draw a line.

6. I then discovered that he'd downloaded it illegally and watched it.

7. I removed his computer and phone. He looked as though he'd been shot.

8. I then had to play Monopoly with him for two and a half hours straight.

9. Then a long walk to the rec to play football for hours in the cold.

10. When he suggested Scrabble I decided we'd had quite enough punishment.

Why I Think I May Be an Evolutionary Cul-de-Sac

1. Small cartons of orange juice for school lunches come in three-packs.

2. Which are very tightly wrapped in cellophane.

3. I normally select a very sharp knife to separate the three cartons.

4. I know that every time I do this I will puncture one of the cartons.

5. And cover myself in orange juice while wasting a perfectly good carton.

6. But every time I am convinced that I am actually a skilled neurosurgeon.

7. Until the point I puncture the carton and cover myself in orange juice.

8. If orange juice were blood, I would be long dead.

9. I am certain that I will never change this tried and tested approach.

10. Because deep down I know that I am a highly skilled neurosurgeon.

Tom's Second Chance at the Big Time

1. The Dads' Soul Choir was making me quietly happy in a noisy way.

2. I don't think I've ever looked forward to Thursdays so much.

3. Then a team of consultants* suggested we enter *Britain's Got Talent*.

4. I said the last thing I needed was to become a national embarrassment.

5. My kids accepted my decision respectfully which is how it should be.

6. Tom called shortly afterwards to suggest the song we should sing.

7. Alan was working on some new moves with Deborah.

8. I got a random email wishing us all the very best of luck.

9. Because it was on the Dads' Soul Choir *BGT* Facebook page.

10. Posted by my kids two days before I made my respected decision.

* My kids.

Why We Nearly Didn't Make It to Our Finest Hour

1. Our coach was held up at the Hangar Lane Gyratory.*

2. Alan got on the coach PA and said he had an announcement to make.

3. Was it 'Caution Vehicle Reversing' by any chance?

4. He said that he was going to ask Deborah out. There was nearly a riot.

5. This was completely out of order. For a start he was married.

6. But apparently his never-seen wife was a figment of his imagination.

7. Then Chris said he was also about to ask Deborah out.

8. Mike said he'd been in love with Deborah from day one.

9. Turns out that we were all in love with Deborah from day one.

10. We agreed that we were all sad and pathetic losers.**

* Which to be honest I always thought was a prototype helicopter.
** But I know that me and Deborah will probably happen. Definitely.

Our Four and a Half Minutes of Fame

1. We were all pretty nervous before the live recording of *BGT*.

2. I convinced myself that it was just a glorified Road Safety Seminar.

3. In front of around 7,000 screaming girls mostly.

4. Deborah got us nicely warmed up but we were all still pretty tense.

5. Then Tom suggested we do some actors' breathing exercises.

6. We were halfway through when Alan started laughing uncontrollably.

7. Soon there was a room full of middle-aged men crying with laughter.

8. We went on and nailed 'Come As You Are', the Beverley Knight classic.

9. Alan needed medical attention afterwards but we were all quite chuffed.*

10. My kids said they were proud. For me that's winning the popular vote.

* Slight understatement. We were like hysterical children.

My Father's Illness, Death and Funeral in 10 Points

1. My dad died of leukaemia, a disease of the little tunnels in the body.

2. It took him so quickly he was gone before we'd got used to him being ill.

3. My mother went into professional hospice mode.

4. I've never seen her smile so much.

5. We buried him in dark, damp earth at the edge of the churchyard.

6. I couldn't help thinking that he'd simply tunnel his way out.

7. A group of French engineers came and said some lovely things about him.

8. Impressive things that he never mentioned at the dinner table.

9. The first time it all really hit home was clearing out his shed.

10. I looked at the boxes of onions all stacked up tidily and I sobbed.

One Thing My Dad Said Which Now Makes Sense

1. Dad always used to talk about the Box in the Loft.

2. This box was to be opened only after his death with the BITL key.

3. We thought it would be his stamp collection which is worth a bit.

4. Pretty much the last thing he said to me was 'Don't forget the box'.

5. The box contained £92,000 in neat £1,000 bundles of cash.

6. Dad had been regularly withdrawing his savings since his diagnosis.

7. There was a note saying to divide it between the kids and not to argue.

8. My sisters insisted on counting the bundles. Every single note.

9. And every single bundle was correct. What did they expect from Dad?

10. Sadly, that's exactly what I expected from them.

What I Have Learned About Sex in 30 Years On and Off

1. In terms of physics, sex is a little bit like gravity only much stronger.

2. It causes random bodies to be massively attracted to each other.

3. Sex takes up less than 1% of actual time and 84% of mental time.

4. A side effect of sex worth being aware of is that it can lead to babies.

5. Nature has arranged it so that no one makes the connection at the time.

6. Sex gets slower but better as you get older. Like rambling.

7. I calculate that I have satisfied 42% of the women I have slept with.*

8. Sexuality is as varied as food and everyone has their own tastes.

9. My sexuality is of the double eggs and chips variety. With tea.

10. Between sex and double egg and chips I know what I fancy most now.

* Satisfaction being measured by awakeness, vital signs, general alertness.

Why I May Not Quite Understand the Whole Gardening Thing

1. When the grass grows I cut it.

2. When bushes grow I trim them.

3. When flowers grow I prune them.

4. Gardening seems a lot like shaving.

5. It's continuous and you have to do it otherwise things look shaggy.

6. Open Gardens are like crack cocaine to my mother.

7. People only open their gardens when they look absolutely immaculate.

8. Instead of overgrown with 10-foot weeds. Which would be better.

9. You would have visitors drooling at the sheer secateurs potential.

10. My garden is like my face. Tidy but with no interesting borders.

Why I Am Now a Bigger Global Celebrity Than Tom Ever Was

1. I am being paid to fly to Finland to make a personal appearance.

2. Finland is a world leader in road safety (and F1 drivers weirdly).

3. They charge people a percentage of their income for speeding fines.

4. So one Finnish millionaire was charged £42,000 for speeding.

5. He now lives in Germany where you can drive like a *verrückten narren*.*

6. I'm going to a Global Highways Regulation Conference. Yes, that's right.

7. Where I am one of the Keynote Speakers. In other words a celebrity.

8. The world is rapidly becoming aware of my Speed Awareness Courses.

9. There is also an exhibition of road safety and signage paraphernalia.

10. I might bring a traffic cone home for Tom. Signed if he's lucky.

* Crazy fool.

Why I Am Grateful to the Japanese for Their Love of Flamenco

1. Helsinki airport is a hub for European flights to Asia.

2. From there you fly over the North Pole. Like Father Christmas.

3. Or Santa-san as they call him in Japan.

4. On my flight home I sat next to a Spanish lady called Lourdes.

5. She was returning from Japan where she had been teaching flamenco.

6. Apparently the Japanese are absolutely obsessed with flamenco.

7. She showed me her dancing class on her phone. Weird but impressive.

8. I told her that I too was a professional dancer. She laughed.

9. I showed her the Dads' Soul Choir on my phone. She laughed again.

10. We agreed to meet up in London so I could show her a few moves.

How I'm Preparing for My Date With Lourdes

1. For a start it's not a date. We're just mature adults meeting for a chat.

2. We're fellow dance professionals meeting as a professional courtesy.

3. So it's not a date. Even though I'm agonising about my trousers.

4. I keep wanting to pull the waist up high, flamenco-style.

5. Not a good look unless you are Antonio Banderas in *Take the Lead*.*

6. I'm also trying to fall out of love before we meet again.

7. Because like a twat I have already fallen half in love.

8. I am an emotional premature ejaculator and I must learn to control it.

9. In fact I don't really like her. I'm just going to be polite.

10. I've bought some new deodorant which smells worse than my armpits.

* 2006 film where he single-handedly proves attractiveness of Latin men.

If I Was Lourdes How I Would Rate Our Date

1. It was a poor choice of restaurant. Although the food was good.

2. Kind of cool facing the open-plan kitchen. Except for the shouting chef.

3. He's a nice guy but far too eccentric for my liking (me not the chef).

4. Very English in that uncool, puppyish, goofy, self-deprecating way.

5. But full marks for talking to me in Spanish – with a Mexican accent.

6. Although virtually every other word was an obscenity.

7. Liked the fact his children are same age as mine. And he loves them.

8. He's a good dad and a nice man but he's no Javier Bardem.

9. I wish he hadn't attempted to do flamenco on our way to the Tube.

10. I think he's in love with me. Probably won't see him again.

If I Was Myself How I Would Rate My Date with Lourdes

1. For a start it wasn't a date. All right it was a date.

2. Poor choice of restaurant. I wanted to stab the chef with his own knife.

3. I'm not completely and utterly in love with Lourdes.

4. She's a very attractive woman obviously. And very sexy.

5. But more importantly she is intelligent and cultured and sharp.

6. Even more importantly than all that she is kind. She listens.

7. Even when I talk shite. Some of which she finds funny. I think.

8. She's a single mum divorced from a Brit nob. Why are there so many?

9. I'd really like to dance with Lourdes. That would be life-changing.

10. I must get Alan to show me some more moves if I can catch him sober.

My Current Standing in the Ongoing Parent vs Screen Contest

1. Screens can't yet cook and the kids can't afford to order takeaway.

2. Screens don't hug them when they get home from school.

3. Screens can't have the mickey taken out of them unlike sad old Dad.

4. Screens often have really unpleasant things on them.

5. Unlike our sofa. Which has me, my paper and my slippers.

6. Screens do have really epic games. That you can play with your mates.

7. Which apparently is better than going for a walk in the fresh air.

8. Unless I power-down the whole house. Which they know I can do.

9. So we hug, eat together, take the mickey and occasionally walk.

10. You won't find that on-screen. Yet.

My Limited Understanding of My Mum's Reaction to My Dad's Death

1. My mother's reaction to my father's death was textbook.

2. Probably because she wrote the textbook on good deaths.

3. For a while it lifted her to an almost saintly level of coping.

4. But when everyone else moved on she started getting really angry.

5. It was as if she felt he'd walked out when she took centre stage.

6. Or he'd only just come up for air and now he was underground again.

7. Or maybe she just didn't want to do the whole tiresome widow thing.

8. Or maybe she found out about a secret Frenchwoman and child.

9. Or maybe it's that old thing that cobblers' children have no shoes.

10. That what you do at work you don't do at home. But I don't know.

Top Sensory Experiences (non-erotic)

1. Building bonfire, setting light to it, kippering yourself in the smoke.

2. Sliding into deep hot bath with tea and Jammie Dodgers on side.

3. Hearing church bells ringing as you walk to Sunday lunch in a pub.

4. Wrapped up in your space blanket after finishing a wall-free marathon.

5. Slipping between crisp, white laundered cotton sheets with clean bod.

6. Sprinting silently down a long narrow hotel corridor.

7. Rolling about on the floor laughing. Preferably on carpet.

8. Galloping (with horse) at full tilt alongside 10 other horses.

9. Hugging your own child and smelling their scalp (under 11 years).

10. A frosted glass of beer after winning a beach volleyball match.*

    * Haven't done it yet but will do before I'm 60.

What's Happened to My Twin Sisters Since I Last Looked

1. Lucy still works in the Aloha 37 years after she started there.

2. What really surprises me is that the restaurant is still going.

3. But they are close to the station and they still do good breakfasts.

4. Charlotte has sold her flat and moved in with Lucy.

5. Neither has a boyfriend but they now have a small dog called Chester.

6. Charlotte has just started working at the Aloha also as a waitress.

7. My mum once told me there was a secret to understanding the twins.

8. Singularly they feel slightly inferior to everyone else.

9. But together they feel slightly superior.

10. Hooee's* chewed remains are all that's left of my relationship with them.

* Leo's cuddly rabbit.

What Charlotte Has Been Doing for the Last 30 Years

1. 1985–1988   Bookkeeper at care home.

2. 1988–1991   Bookkeeper at care home.

3. 1991–1994   Bookkeeper at care home.

4. 1994–1997   Bookkeeper at care home.

5. 1997–2000   Bookkeeper at care home.

6. 2000–2003   Bookkeeper at care home.

7. 2003–2006   Explored Polynesia with Swedish lesbian yachtswoman.

8. 2006–2009   Bookkeeper at care home.

9. 2009–2012   Bookkeeper at care home.

10. 2012–2015   Bookkeeper at care home.

How My Work Turned Out to Be Entertainment and Competence

1. I run one Speed Awareness Course a week just to keep up to speed.

2. The rest of the time I look after the business.

3. We now offer other courses like British Citizenship and Deradicalisation.

4. I'm seriously thinking of running a Marriage Guidance Course.

5. I'm not sure if it would be run by 'Happily Married' or 'Happily Divorced'.

6. And then most weekends we have a Dads' Soul Choir gig.

7. We each earn about £50 for these which doesn't really cover the petrol.

8. We also have groupies. Mostly woman of a certain age.

9. I've never been sure what a certain age means. But they're very nice.

10. I could fall in love every night. But I don't because I'm quietly happy.

Why Loving Lourdes Is Easy (Because She's Beautiful*)

1. We both have kids. We don't have to worry about breeding.

2. We've been bruised by marriage so we won't be rushing back up the aisle.

3. Lourdes is kind. Which I've learned is just about the most important thing.

4. But she also happens to be the sexiest woman alive. Which is a bonus.

5. We talk in Spanish which filters out a lot of the bollocks I talk.

6. But not the obscenities. So she gets quite crude pleasantness.

7. Which makes her laugh. We seem to do a lot of laughing.

8. I never knew relationships could be this relaxed. I'm not working at it.

9. I've noticed I've stopped falling in love with anyone else.

10. I am not learning flamenco. I'm leaving that to the Japanese.

* Minnie Riperton – 'Lovin' You'.

What Life Has Taught Me So Far

1. Not to trust any emotions before eating.

2. There is nothing to dislike about a tree.

3. We are the biggest and smallest thing in the universe.

4. Every day is a boring procession of unimaginable miracles.

5. There is a pattern to life but not one you'd want as wallpaper.

6. Love is the only thing really worth having.

7. Character will out eventually.

8. Not everyone gets the karmic spanking they deserve.

9. Showers are for showering.

10. Life is beautifully and invisibly engineered.

Why Autumn Is Probably My Favourite Season

1. There is absolutely no compulsion to be having a wonderful holiday.

2. You can put on your brushed-cotton sheets and 13-tog winter duvet.

3. Even if you have to take them off again because you're incredibly hot.

4. Conkers. Lovely word, beautiful things.

5. Christmas is still far enough away to be a pleasant prospect.

6. Pubs light their fires.

7. Roasts happen every Sunday. Salads can be forgotten for 10 months.

8. The kids are back at school and have plenty of homework.

9. You feel you've worked late even when you leave at five.

10. Weak sunlight on golden leaves makes me feel pleasantly *weltschmerzy*.

Why For the First Time I Feel Like Giving Up Lists

1. Looking back it seems I've always written lists when I'm alone.

2. Trying to pin down experiences which have been a bit too much for me.

3. Lists have made things more manageable, given them structure.

4. But they're not usually written when laughing with friends.

5. Or walking with the woman I love.

6. Or feeling a warm wind arrive from the south.

7. 'Happiness writes white,' they say. It speaks for itself.

8. So now I want to put my pen down.

9. Because my life is growing through the bullet points.

10.

Guy Browning is CEO of Smokehouse,
a global training consultancy. He lives quietly
In Oxfordshire with his three children.

Acknowledgements

A small handful of people have been enormously helpful in the putting together of *My Life in Lists* – slightly too few to list.

Firstly, thank you to the very special Rosemary Davidson at Square Peg. She encouraged me to keep writing when it was only a few bullet points and then guided it through to become a hell of a lot of bullet points. So thank you very much to Rosemary and to her unrivalled production team of Lindsay Nash, Kathy Fry and Sarah-Jane Forder.

Thanks also to my legendary agent Juliet Mushens and also Nathalie Hallam whose beautiful contracts are actually longer than this book.

Peter White, a Jenson Interceptor of a man, taught me everything I know about electrical engineering, which is a tiny percentage of what he knows.

A very big thank you to Ana Pampin who shared with me the secrets of Spanish and flamenco.

Tom Mitchelson's faith in this book has been unwavering – small but unwavering. But he has helped me with insights into all sorts of things about which I knew nothing.

Finally, I'd like to acknowledge Janet Brown. Legendary cartoonist, art director and designer and also the brilliant illustrator of this book. Thank you.